BINDS
OF THE
FORSAKEN

ELIJAH HER

Binds of the Forsaken
Copyright © 2025 by Elijah Her
All rights reserved

This book is a work of fiction. Names, characters, businesses, organizations, places, events, and incidents are either creations of the author's imagination or used fictitiously. Any resemblance to actual persons, living or deceased, or real events or locations, is purely coincidental.

Cover Design: Elijah Her
Interior Art: Canva
Cover & Title Page Art: rummkt / rummpt

Second Edition
ISBN: 979-8-9927299-0-0 (paperback)
ISBN: 979-8-9927299-1-7 (ebook)

F90 PRESS

www.f90press.com

To the readers who long to see a character take 'I'll find you in every lifetime'

as a promise, not just a sentiment.

CONTENT NOTES

Binds of the Forsaken includes explicit sexual content. It also touches on themes some may be sensitive to or find triggering:

Frequent references to death, loss, and the emotional toll of witnessing repeated deaths of a loved one. Depictions of organized crime, physical violence, and murder. Struggle with trauma related to past lives, god like figures, familial pressure, and past child abuse. Societal pressures regarding queer relationships, and external homophobia.

PRONUNCIATION GUIDE

Aither *(EYE-thur)*
Daimon *(DYE-mon)*
Erebos *(EH-reh-bos)*
Eudaimon *(YOU-dye-mon)*
Kakodaimon *(KAK-oh-dye-mon)*
Khaos *(KAY-os)*
Philetos *(fee-LEE-tos)*
Silas *(SIGH-lus)*
Theion *(THAY-on)*
Vassallo *(vah-SAHL-loh)*
Zayd *(ZAY-d)*

Prologue

"Philetos."

The name broke from me, thin as breath, and vanished into the void.

My wings burned, every muscle straining as I fell. The glow of the Aither dimmed above me, receding into distance until it was no more than a pale ember swallowed by the dark.

"Philetos."

Tears rose, drifting upward instead of falling, defying gravity's pull as the mists of Khaos gathered beneath me. I closed my eyes. Failure pressed down heavier than the abyss.

The gods, the Theion were meant to be both shadow and light, cruel and kind in equal measure. But in that moment, all I could feel was the silence of their absence.

My only crime had been love. A mortal's soul—my charge, my beloved. And I had failed him.

"Philetos."

The word tore from me in a gasp as my fall halted. Blood filled my mouth, iron-salt thick on my tongue. My hands, trembling, found the shard of metal buried deep in my abdomen. Breath faltered. The scent of my own blood clung to the air.

I tried to rise, but the weakness held fast, heavy as chains. Above me, the Aither's light was veiled, unreachable, and I—unworthy.

Suspended in the colorless void, I drifted between agony and silence. Once, Khaos had been a haven for Daimons. Now it was only a prison, timeless and cold. Through its shifting fog, I caught faint glimpses of the mortal world—people walking unknowing, untouched by the horror that lay just beyond their realm.

A shadow stirred. A figure moved toward me, form blurred in the haze. It had been centuries since I had seen another Daimon. Punishment, perhaps, sent by the Theion.

My vision wavered, but I reached out, desperate, bloodied fingers aching for the warmth I remembered—soft blond hair, eyes that glowed like embers. *Agápi mou.* My love.

Philetos.

The name reverberated in me, but when my hand found purchase, it met not warmth but hard flesh, cold as stone.

The shadow sharpened. A towering creature, horns rising from its brow, gray eyes gleaming silver in the dark. Clawed hands closed around me, not with violence, but with a strange, unsettling gentleness.

One arm slipped beneath my knees, the other against my back. The shard shifted inside me. White-hot pain surged, ripping a cry from my throat. My body arched in agony as the wound tore open—then knit together, nerve by nerve, bone by bone, a healing as brutal as the injury had been.

The creature's chest was cold against me, but steady. The pain ebbed, leaving only exhaustion in its wake.

I forced my eyes open. The blur cleared, and I saw it for what it was.

A Kakodaimon.

Why would one of darkness heal me? Where could it be taking me?

Confusion pressed against the edges of my mind as consciousness slipped like a tide.

Chapter One

Zayd

The music swelled and filled the space around me, but it was more than just sound. It was a thread, golden and delicate, that wound its way through the fibers of my being, tugging at memories long buried. His voice—it wasn't just a sound, but a touch, a presence that brushed against the edges of divinity itself. Each note seemed to shimmer in the air, as if plucked from the Aither. Among the Eudaimons, we believed that art, true art, was the work of the Theion. A gift from the gods. And when Silas sang, I could feel that connection, that gift, coursing through him.

In every life, his voice had held that power. In this life, it was no different, yet somehow it was more. The richness to it, a depth that tugged at something deeper within me. This form, Silas, was closer to Philetos than I had ever seen in the past. His voice, his stature, even the way his golden hair tumbled messily over his forehead, begging to be swept back—everything about him mirrored my long-lost love. His eyes, though, were the true link to the past: deep, earthy brown with flecks of gold that sparkled when they caught the light, like embers glowing beneath a darkened surface. There was a warmth in them, a familiarity, that always called to me.

And yet, in this life, he was different in ways to be expected. This life had shaped him in many ways. The way he spoke was rougher, his manner more guarded. Tattoos and scars marred the canvas of his body, evidence of the life he had lived so far. It was a new story, a new life.

"Do you ever tire of watching him from the shadows of Khaos?" The voice beside me was a soft intrusion, pulling me out of my thoughts. Eryx. His presence, always so bold, had slipped in unnoticed this time, though I should have sensed it. His arrival was never subtle, nor were his words.

"I'm not watching," I muttered, though even as the words left my mouth, I knew they were a lie. My gaze hadn't left Silas for a moment, my heart pulled, as it always was, toward the familiar flame. Three thousand years of watching, waiting. I had seen Philetos in many forms—man and woman, soft and hardened, calm and stormy. Yet at the center of it all, it was always him. My soul knew his, was drawn to him, no matter the shell. No matter the life.

Eryx chuckled, sliding into the booth across from me. "Watching, lurking, stalking—call it what you will." His gray eyes gleamed, sharp as they fixed on me. He was everything I was not. Where I was quiet, he was loud; where I held back, he surged forward, unafraid to take what he wanted from this world. And yet, despite the differences, he remained. Whether it was loyalty, amusement, or some other, darker motivation. Perhaps it was pity, if Kakodaimons were even capable of such a thing. I had long ceased to question why he stayed at my side.

My eyes drifted back to Silas. Even through the muted tones of the Khaos, the world that shrouded me in shades of gray and black, his beauty shone. His voice carried, wrapping around me like an embrace. From that small wooden stage in the corner of his modest bar, he glowed—a beacon in the dullness of my existence.

"I am trying something different," I said, my voice soft, almost as if the words were meant more for myself than for him. "I plan to let him live out this life without me."

Eryx's laugh was a low, throaty thing, full of disbelief. "Oh yeah? " He leaned in, his voice dropping to a conspiratorial whisper. "It will always end the same regardless. Philetos is mortal." His gaze flicked to Silas as he stepped off the stage, his smile warm and easy as the small crowd clapped and cheered. "So why not take what you want, instead of brooding."

I swallowed hard, my eyes tracing the lines of Silas' face, the familiar curve of his lips. The crowd adored him. How could they not? He had distanced himself from the darkness of his family, from the blood and the violence that came with the name Vassallo. He had made a life of his own, a quiet life. A peaceful life. He deserved this peace, deserved to live without me, without the weight of our bond pulling him back into the cycle of pain and loss that had followed us through centuries.

"I don't want to take this happiness from him." I whispered. "He's worked hard for this."

Eryx's gaze softened, a rare thing for him. His voice, too, lost some of its sharpness. "And what of your own happiness, Zayd?" His hand briefly brushed against mine, warm, grounding, pulling me out of the haze of my thoughts. "You've tried this before." He trailed off, shaking his head with a knowing smile. "You know you can't help yourself."

He was right. Of course, he was right. I had tried, time and again, to step back, to let Philetos live without interference. But always, always I was drawn back to him. The bond between us, forged by the Theion themselves, was a thing of fate, of inevitability. To resist it was to resist the very order of the cosmos.

His long fingers raked through his ashy hair, his eyes glinting with a mixture of curiosity and amusement. Eryx had chosen his form carefully, his large frame and sculpted features designed to lure mortals in. A defined jawline, broad shoulders, and a wicked glint in his gray eyes made him seem both angelic and dangerous. By contrast, I felt dulled—once angelic myself, but now stripped of that radiance.

"Why are you here, anyway? Don't you have some misfortune to spread?" I said softly, my gaze lingering on Silas as he moved behind the bar, laughing with a patron. His smile was like sunlight breaking through clouds, too bright, too warm for me to touch.

"I've made my quota for the night." Eryx's grin was sharp, flashing his canines. His voice dropped, teasing, flirty.

"Besides, it's much more fun to tempt you into something... sinful, my little Eudai." His eyes gleamed with mischief, the lazy, predatory smile curling across his lips. He leaned in slightly, his broad shoulders shifting as if to draw me closer, his gaze lingering on my face in a way that was all too familiar.

I rolled my eyes, though the gesture lacked conviction. I'd sought comfort in Eryx before, in fleeting moments of loneliness and yearning. Though my heart belonged to Philetos, I had found solace in other arms over the centuries—both mortal and not. There were times when I tried to live without him, to ignore the tie, to fall in love with others, but it was always futile. No matter how hard I tried, our souls were always drawn back together, and when we met, the flames consumed us once more.

Eryx's hand slid across the table, his fingers brushing lightly against my jaw. His thumb traced the line of my chin, slowly, deliberately, his touch both intimate and commanding. "You need a distraction," he said, his voice dropping to a whisper that curled around me like smoke. His gaze flicked to my lips, his thumb brushing over them lightly. There was something new in his eyes now, something I couldn't place, but the way he looked at me made my heart quicken, though not in the same way Philetos always had.

Before I could respond, he grasped my hand, pulling me to my feet. As we walked through the bar, I could feel his intention. The bathroom—of course. It was seedy, dirty, exactly the kind of place Eryx reveled in. His form shifted from the Khaos, becoming solid, corporeal, and I followed suit. The world of color and sound rushed back in around us as we reentered the mortal realm.

My gaze flicked to Silas one last time. He was standing behind the bar, his smile gentle as he poured a drink for a customer. He was beautiful, so tempting that I almost wanted to reach out to him. But before the thought could linger, Eryx pulled me into the bathroom, closing the door behind us with a soft click.

In an instant, Eryx's body pressed against mine, his hand cupping the side of my face while the other rested firmly at my hip. His nose grazed along my jawline, the intimate gesture sending a ripple through me. My breath became shallow, and I whispered, "Eryx," His name escaped me before I could stop it, my voice barely more than a breath. My hand moved up to grip his tattooed arm, feeling the warmth of his skin beneath my fingers. I pulled him closer.

I could feel him everywhere. His hands glided over my body with a familiarity that shouldn't exist and yet it did. I wasn't sure when we had crossed the line—when the simmering tension between us had finally ignited—but there was no turning back. There was too much history between us now. The fire that simmered between us was undeniable, but it never went beyond this—these stolen moments of lust and distraction.

Kakodaimons and Eudaimons weren't meant to mix like this. Normally, we were at odds—light against dark. We were meant to guide and protect, while they caused misfortune, beckoned temptation. But I had long since strayed from the divine mandate that forbade us from seeking pleasure, from forming attachments that went beyond the platonic, whether with mortals or fellow Daimons. That, among other reasons, was why I had been forsaken by the Theion and cast out of Aither.

Eryx, for all his brashness, was my only constant besides Philetos. But Philetos... Philetos never remembered me. With each life he began anew, his memories wiped clean. I alone carried the burden of our past, while he lived in blissful ignorance.

"You're doing it again, Zayd," Eryx murmured, his voice a low, gentle command. "Focus on me." His lips pressed against mine, coaxing me back into the present moment. His hand slipped from my hip, fingers moving with expert ease as they undid the buckle of my belt, sliding my trousers down to rest just below my hips.

"So eager," I murmured against his lips, feeling the warmth of his body press closer.

"I didn't bring you in here to talk," he replied, his tone laced with a wicked edge.

My head tipped back as his hand closed around my cock, stroking slowly, teasingly. His thumb grazed over the sensitive tip, sending sharp waves of pleasure through my body. My heart pounded in my chest, so loud I was sure he could hear it. I tried to steady my breathing, but it came out in shallow gasps, betraying how badly I was falling apart under his touch.

I reached up, tangling my fingers in his ashy hair, pulling him into me further. The kiss that followed was desperate and primal. It was all-consuming, a violent clash of want and frustration, and I lost myself in it, in him. I needed this. I needed to forget, even if just for a moment.

Eryx dropped to his knees, his hands gripping my hips as he looked up at me with a predatory gleam. There was something twistedly beautiful about seeing a Kakodai like this, kneeling before me, his perfectly sculpted features framed by the flickering, ugly yellow light of the bathroom. His dark, tailored clothes hugged his muscular frame, a contrast to the filth of the setting. It was as though he relished the degradation of it all.

He leaned forward, his lips brushing against the tip of my arousal before his mouth opened, taking me inside. A groan escaped my throat, my fingers sliding to cradle his face as he worked his tongue along my shaft. The sensation of his hot, wet mouth made me momentarily forget the dingy surroundings—the overwhelming air freshener, the flickering light, the muffled conversations and music from the bar outside. I could almost forget about Silas... almost.

I felt the tension coil low in my stomach, a molten heat pooling and building with each movement of Eryx's mouth. My hands slid to the sides of his head, gently guiding him, pushing him deeper as my length throbbed within the tight confines of his throat. His eyes met mine, dark gray meeting stormy blue, and I felt my face flush under his gaze. I had always hated when he looked at me like that—like I was something worthy of admiration.

The release hit me like a wave crashing through my body, taking me under with it. A low groan escaped my lips, his name caught in my throat as I let go completely, everything else dissolving into nothing. With a final thrust, the pressure in my sack snapped, release spilling down his throat in hot, pulsing waves.

My chest rose and fell rapidly as I tried to steady my breathing as I slumped against the wall. Eryx pulled back slowly, wiping the sheen of saliva from his chin with the back of his hand before standing, his expression one of smug satisfaction. I know that was him holding back, that he wanted to unravel with me.

A knock at the door jolted me back to reality. "Anyone in there?" a voice called from the other side.

I barely had a moment to react before Eryx's lips were on mine again, silencing any response. His kiss tasted of salty musk, my release still lingering on his tongue. "Eryx," I mumbled, pushing further against the wall, trying to break free from the moment.

He relented forcibly, chuckling darkly as I escaped him and went into the Khaos. "You're no fun." He unlocked the door and faded into the mists, his form becoming incorporeal as he vanished from the mortal realm to join me. We both stood silent for a moment, watching as a drunken human stumbled inside, oblivious to what had transpired.

I straightened my clothes, tucking in my shirt and adjusting my pants. "It would have been risky if we continued," I muttered, feeling the tension drain from my body. If the human had asked Silas to unlock the bathroom door... I didn't want to imagine the complicated feelings that would emerge inside of me.

Eryx shrugged, leaning casually against the wall. "I enjoy a little risk."

I ignored his comment, stepping out of the bathroom and back into the dimly lit bar. My gaze immediately scanned the room, searching for Silas. But I couldn't see him.

"Did your human leave already?" Eryx asked, his voice teasing as he trailed behind me.

"No," I said quietly, the familiar tug of our soul bond pulling me in the right direction. "He's still here."

That was the constant, the tether that always existed between us. I could feel Philetos, always, as if an invisible thread connected our souls. It is forged the instant he is reincarnated and remains unbroken until the moment of his death.

The bond pulsed with intensity, tightening as the distance between us shrank. Without a word, I followed its pull, Eryx trailing close behind. The muffled hum of the bar faded into the night as we stepped into the fresh air, heading for the back alley. With each step, the connection between us strengthened, drawing me toward him. The low thrum of voices broke through the quiet, tense and angry, growing louder as I neared. My heart quickened, the weight in my chest growing heavier with every footfall.

Before I saw them, I heard them—the rough, gravelly voices of two men confronting Silas, though the exact words were still lost in the haze of Khaos.

When I rounded the corner, they came into view: two hulking figures, their skin inked with tattoos that spoke of violence and allegiance. A symbol on one man's hand—a mark of a gang, tied to the mafia but not one I recognized—caught my attention. They towered over Silas, their postures threatening, their energy radiating danger. One of them shifted, his coat lifting just enough to reveal a glint of metal. A gun, unmistakable, tucked into the waistband of his slacks.

Silas stood his ground, arms crossed tightly over his chest in a posture of forced indifference. But I knew better. His fingers dug into his biceps, tension radiating from his frame. His eyes blazed with a fire that betrayed his calm facade, a readiness to fight simmering just below the surface.

I felt Eryx before his hand touched my shoulder, his presence now like an icy breath against my skin. He was always the shadow at my side, a constant reminder of the boundaries I shouldn't cross. His grip was firm but not harsh, a wordless restraint.

"You don't have permission from the Theion to intervene with fate," he whispered, his tone a mix of caution and amusement.

I didn't look at him. My eyes remained locked on Silas, on the way his jaw clenched, the small shifts in his stance as he braced himself for what was to come. That gun, the barely contained rage—it would only take a single misstep for everything to spiral out of control.

"When has that ever stopped me when it came to Philetos?" I muttered, my voice low. I would go through any lengths for him—regardless of the consequences.

With a sharp shrug, I shook off Eryx's hand and stepped forward, slipping free of Khaos. The world around me sharpened—the cool night air hit my skin, and the dim light from a flickering streetlamp cast long shadows over the alley. The scene before me came into sharp focus, but the men were still unaware of my presence, too wrapped up in their confrontation with Silas to notice my approach.

Chapter Two

Silas

The night air was calm, cool, the kind that makes you think maybe—just maybe—you could have peace for once. Then the dumpster lid slammed, and peace went to hell. Voices followed, Irish and smug, the kind of sound that makes your teeth itch.

"You know, Liam, he looks a lot like Cesare's son, doesn't he?"

Great. Name-dropping my father meant they actually knew who I was. Lucky me.

"Yeah, heard he was an ungrateful brat. Shirked all his responsibilities."

I shut the lid gently, turned, and plastered on a grin. Hands wide, like I was hosting a game show. "So what's the plan, lads? Stand around critiquing my family tree, or actually try to kill me? Because I gotta say, your foreplay's weak."

That earned me a flash of irritation, and irritation was good. Irritated men got sloppy.

They were big, block-headed types—the kind who thought leather jackets and slick suits counted as personality. One scratched at his neck, and the tattoo glared back: dagger with a Celtic cross. *Callaghan.* Because of course.

"You're a long way from L.A.," I said, folding my arms. "Please tell me you didn't drive all this way just for me. I'm flattered, really, but flowers would've been cheaper."

Leather Jacket sneered. "Surprised to find you here. Shouldn't you be with your family, for your da's funeral? Or did you not care enough to leave your cozy little bartender life?"

The words hit harder than I expected. My father—dead? No call, no word. And August? God, what about August?

"Ah, the gears are turning now," he taunted. "Callaghan wants the heirs cut out before one of ye can step up to the Legare throne."

My jaw locked. So that was it. They were here to take me out. And if they were here, August might already be—

No. Don't think about it.

I forced a smirk. "Does this look like the face of a guy campaigning for boss? I run a bar, lads. Mafia succession isn't really on my to-do list. Right between 'order limes' and 'fix the damn ice machine.'"

Movement flickered at the edge of my vision. Another man. *Shit.* How many were waiting?

They glanced toward the distraction, and that was all I needed. My fist drove into the suited one's gut. He folded like a bad poker hand, and my knee found his groin. A grunt, a curse, and I didn't stop—one hand on the back of his head, my knee slamming up, bone crunching under the rhythm. Once, twice, four times. By the end he looked less like a man and more like a Picasso painting.

I let him drop, breath ragged, blood warm on my jeans. "Hey, free nose job. You're welcome, pal."

Then I heard it—the slick, unmistakable click of a chambered round.

"You langer!" Leather Jacket spat, gun leveled right at me.

I froze, staring down the barrel, waiting for the bang, the burn, the blackout. Instead—*crack*. Not a gunshot. Bone. The guy dropped like a marionette with his strings cut.

I blinked. My brain caught up about two beats late. Standing over him wasn't another Callaghan thug—it was... well, not what I expected. Clean-cut, tailored suit, dark hair so perfect I wanted to mess it up just to prove it was real. No ink, no scars, not even a wrinkle in his shirt. He looked like he'd wandered out of a Fortune 500 meeting and into my alley.

And yet he was staring at me like I'd just kicked his dog.

"You alright?" His voice cracked a little, concern tangled with something else I couldn't name. "You're not hurt, are you?"

I just... stared. Too long. Definitely too long. Something about him—it tugged at me, like deja vu with teeth. Familiar, but impossible. My chest stuttered in the stupid way teenage boys do when their crush looks at them, and yeah, I hated that.

I shook it off, scanning him for anything relating to my past life. Nothing. No weapon, no mark, no grit. Which left two options: unlucky passerby, or worse—one of my regulars. My stomach sank. Ivy was still inside holding down the fort.

I probably looked like an idiot, mouth half open, so I forced a chuckle. "Not even a scratch. You should see the other guy." My eyes flicked to the bloody mess on the pavement. "On second thought, maybe don't."

He didn't laugh. Just looked down, jaw tight, his hand brushing his chest. That's when it clicked—no bruising. He had knocked that guy out with a blow that should have bruised, but here he was without so much as a scratch. No swelling, no split skin. What the hell was he?

And why did it feel like I knew him?

"You... want a drink? For your troubles?" My voice came out lighter than I meant, like I was trying not to spook him. Which was insane, considering he'd just folded a grown man like laundry.

He hesitated, dark eyes flicking back the way he came before landing on me again. Finally: "Alright... yeah, I'll take that drink." The smile didn't reach his eyes.

I nodded, hoping it looked casual. Blood was soaking through my jeans, sticky and hot, and I knew I was grinning like a lunatic. I always did after a fight. Adrenaline was my worst tell. Had he noticed? Is that why he looked like he'd rather bolt than follow me in? I needed to smooth this over before word got around that the local bartender moonlighted as a bone grinder.

"Go on inside. I'll catch up after I call the cops about these two idiots. Pathetic drunks, thought they could rob someone in an alley. Can you believe it?" I rolled my eyes, selling it harder than I felt. It was the first lie that came to mind.

He slipped inside. I pulled out my phone. It rang once.

"Mr. Vassallo, what do I owe the pleasure?"

"Couple of Callaghans tried to jump me. I'm guessing it has to do with my father." I hesitated. No, Cesare couldn't be dead. He was old, sure, but healthy, protected. "Two down. Address is—"

"I'll send men." Arnaldo's voice cut like a blade. "And Silas... it's time to come home."

My chest tightened. He was right. I had to go back. "Miss me already, Arnaldo?"

"Come home, or I'll send someone to make you."

I let out a low chuckle. "I'll take that as a yes."

The line died. I shook my head, tucking the phone away with a smile I didn't feel. Shrugging off my flannel, I wrapped it around one of their guns and squeezed off two muffled shots. The shirt went in the dumpster. The gun on the body. Nice and tidy.

Standing at the threshold of the bar's back entrance, I let out a long breath and glanced back at the bodies cooling in the alley. I should've known the quiet wouldn't last. Peace was a fairy tale, and I was an idiot for pretending otherwise.

My hand drifted to my chest, fingertips brushing the fabric, tracing muscle out of habit. And there it was again—that stupid flutter, like my heart hadn't gotten the memo we were done with surprises tonight. I snorted under my breath. "Great. Catching feelings in a murder alley. Real healthy, Silas."

The bar's atmosphere washed over me like a second skin. The radio hummed low through the speakers, some local station playing a mix of old rock. The air carried that familiar cocktail of liquor, beer, and too many stories spilled over wood and glass. Five years I'd been here. A new town. A name unknown. A new me. Call it starting over. Call it hiding. Either way, it worked—most days.

My fingers trailed along the counter as I moved behind the bar, tying an apron low around my hips. The knot was loose, sloppy—more for cover than function. With luck, anyone catching a glimpse of the dark patch on my jeans would just assume I'd lost a fight with a spilled merlot.

And there he was. My mystery savior. The clean-cut knight who dropped in from nowhere and cracked a skull like it was nothing. He sat at the bar, knuckles propped against his cheek, lost in some private storm. He looked up only when I leaned in.

"What's your poison?" I asked, aiming for casualness. "Cocktails, beer, wine? Or are you more of a non-alcoholic guy?" The chuckle I added was forced, but smooth enough. Better to keep him talking about drinks than, ask, "are the police here yet?"

He hesitated, long enough that I caught myself studying him harder than I meant to. His expression was... heavy. Sorrowful, maybe. And hell, I wasn't one to judge, but it pulled me in. "You okay?" I asked, softer this time.

His smile flickered—half-hearted—as he straightened. "Yeah. Sorry. Just... so many choices."

"You look like a prosecco guy," I said with a tilt of my head, pretending to size him up. "How about an Aperol Spritz? Bubbly, bright—good cover for a brooding type. If you don't like it, you can toss it. On the house either way."

His lips curved into something genuine this time, small but enough to make my chest tighten. "I do enjoy prosecco."

Fuck, he is handsome.

"On the house? Wow, you must be important." Ivy's voice cut in from behind me. She appeared with a tray stacked full of glassware, blowing a stubborn strand of red hair out of her eyes.

I shot her a look, then turned back to him with a grin, tossing him a wink. "Oh, he's important, alright. Helped me take out some garbage earlier."

Ivy blinked, brows knitting, but I let the half-joke hang there. She rolled with it, smiling anyway. "Garbage buddies, huh? What's your name? Don't think I've seen you around before."

That was Ivy—always digging, always curious. Arroyo Grande was small enough that if someone sneezed downtown, half the town caught the rumor before the tissue hit the trash. She'd probably be searching this guy's socials before the night was over, sending me screenshots and winks. She meant well—always trying to push me into dating, especially if someone remotely attractive walked in.

But dating meant questions. Questions meant answers. And answers led straight back to a family name I'd buried. Better to stay behind the bar, pouring drinks and dodging bullets, than let anyone get close enough to peel the label off.

I slid the finished drink across the bar, glass catching in the light before it stopped in front of him. Leaning on my forearms, the old wood creaked like it wanted in on the conversation. I'd be lying if I said I wasn't curious who he was. Those eyes—dark, stormy blue—were the kind of eyes that made you wonder what they'd seen. And, if I was being honest, the kind of eyes I wanted to see staring back at me from my sheets.

"Zayd," he said finally, after a long sip. No grimace, no hesitation. Just a double take at the glass before he went in for more. That was bartender code for *nailed it.*

"I'm here for the South County Historical Society. Big push to preserve the old mission in San Luis Obispo," he added, setting the drink down.

"Glad someone's paying attention to it," I said, keeping my tone casual. "Beautiful place. You've been by already?"

He shook his head. "Not yet. Just got into town tonight."

"Really?" Ivy piped up, leaning closer like she'd been waiting for her cue. "It's a must-see. Silas could show you around, you know—get the somewhat-local's tour." Her smirk was sharp enough to cut glass.

I laughed, though heat crawled up my neck. I should've seen it coming—hell, I did see it coming. Normally I brushed her off, but this time... well, this time was different.

"Yeah, I could show you," I said, eyes catching his again. "If you're free."

"I'm not busy tomorrow."

"Tomorrow it is," I said, voice lighter than I meant it to be. "Meet here. Ten work?"

Ivy bumped me with her hip, grin wide. "It's a date then."

I let out another laugh, shaking my head. "Yeah. A date." The word tasted strange on my tongue, like something I hadn't said in years.

A young couple at the far end of the bar waved me over, breaking the moment. I gave Zayd one last smile—quick, private—before peeling myself away.

Chapter Three

Zayd

What was that? The instant our eyes had met, I felt it—the sharp snap of our bond, like a string pulled too tight suddenly thrumming back to life.

I drifted closer to where Silas lay, his mortal body surrendered to the quiet rhythm of sleep. His breath rose and fell, steady, fragile, achingly human. I reached out, brushing my fingers against the curve of his temple, but there was nothing—no warmth, no resistance. The veil of Khaos lay between us, unyielding, untouchable. He did not stir, not even a flicker of recognition.

That bond, that tether, it had been forged with Philetos' death and with every reincarnation it had returned, only to break again when death claimed him. But this time... it had broken prematurely. He was not dead. He was not dying. Could it be? Had the Fates, so merciless for centuries, shown mercy at last? Had the Theion relented, loosened their grip on their punishment, after all these years?

Nearly three millennia had slipped past me—more than fifteen lives, each shorter than the last, each ending before I could hold him long enough. Lifetimes dissolving like sand through my hands. And now, here, now—*why now?* What had shifted in the weave of the world?

Hope stirred within me, perilous and intoxicating. What if this was the beginning? What if this time, we might exist without the shattering end, without the tearing apart? Always before, as soon as Philetos began to feel the bond, our love, the world conspired to rip him from me. But perhaps—just perhaps—this was different.

Two centuries had passed since I last stood this close to one of his reincarnations, since another final breath, and since silence had swallowed me whole again. And now here he was, Silas—bearing the echo of that first form, of Philetos, even down to the cadence of his voice, so cruelly familiar. Hope rose again, a dangerous flame licking at the edges of me. Was it a sign? Was this the life where we would finally finish what we began? Or would the Theion drag me back into the same endless grief?

My thoughts returned again and again to the alley. The men who had appeared there—it made no sense. Silas had walked away from that world, severed himself from the life he was born into. So why now? What did they want?

I sank to my knees beside his bed, my arms folding across the edge of the mattress, my chin resting against them as I let my gaze linger on him. He had turned in his sleep, his body curled slightly toward me, one arm tucked beneath the pillow. Peaceful. Vulnerable. So different from the man I had seen only hours ago, standing in defiance of shadows that would have devoured him.

He was twenty-five when he abandoned Legare. When he abandoned Cesare Vassallo—his father in name only, never in truth. There had been no paternal warmth in Cesare, no love. Only ambition. Only cruelty.

Cesare had carved him into a weapon. Disposal. Cleanup. A blade meant to silence whatever loose ends threatened the family.

But I remembered before that—when he was younger. How he could light a room simply by stepping into it, his eyes alive with hope, sweetness, something so bright it almost hurt to look at. Alessia had tried to keep Cesare's darkness at bay, to shelter her sons from its reach. But Silas was the eldest. The heir. He was the first the darkness chose. It wrapped itself around him, twisted him until even his light became something terrible and beautiful in its own way. Not the kind that inspired hope, but the kind you met at the end of your breath, when regret was the last thing to pass your lips.

And then... he left.

He built something else. Found something that was his. I saw it in his eyes again, that light returning—fragile but alive—when he was behind the bar, when music filled the air, when he laughed with the people who surrounded him. He had begun to inspire again, not through fear, but through life. Through joy.

My hand slipped past the veil of Khaos, crossing the boundary of our realms. The back of my fingers traced the curve of his cheek, reverent, as though touching something sacred. "Philetos," I whispered. My hand drifted into his hair, silken and pliable beneath my touch. His lips curved faintly into a smile—gentle, unknowing. A dream-born response, but enough to undo me all the same.

My hand slipped back into Khaos, vanishing beneath me once more, and the mortal world thinned around me. I should leave. I hadn't meant to lie to Silas earlier. Lies always tangled, always festered—but sometimes they were necessary. Protection demanded them. His mind, his body... mortals were fragile in ways they never realized until it was too late.

And yet, I was tired of it. Tired of lying to every version of him. Tired of hiding myself, of dimming my affections, of dressing truth in shadows just to keep him safe. The weight of centuries was heavy enough; the pretense only made it heavier.

Some lies were small, trivial, but they still lodged in my head like splinters. Most of my kind had adapted, keeping step with the times as though centuries were no different than passing seasons. But I had not. I still moved in half-steps, too slow for the world that kept remaking itself around me.

Now there was the matter of that excuse I had given—the South County Historical Society, the old mission in San Luis Obispo. A place I'd only seen mentioned on a flyer not long ago, a historic site turned into a convenient shield for the reasoning of my presence. Now I would have to research it, trace its history, if only to make the lie real enough to stand.

I had never been skilled at this—at weaving lives that weren't mine. That had always been Eryx's strength. He lived among mortals with ease, his lies seamless, his roles believable. He made masks look like second skins. I, on the other hand... I was not built for such things. I was forsaken, yes, but Eudaimon. Made for reverence, for devotion, not for deception. And every time I played at it, I felt the fault lines widening inside me.

Every line widened and crossed, every pit dug deeper into shadow, was worth it—because it led me back to him. To Philetos.

Chapter Four

Silas

I sat in my car outside the Grove & Grain, engine humming under me, staring at the painted sign that really needed a touch-up. My eyes were on it, but I wasn't actually seeing it. My head was still caught in the dream.

White pillars had stretched up into a sky too pale to be anything but dawn, marble glowing like it had never aged a day. Curtains—sheets, whatever they were—hung from the columns, swaying in a lazy breeze. The whole place smelled like jasmine, thick enough to cling to my lungs. Somewhere in the background, water trickled, slow and steady, like a fountain I couldn't quite see.

I'd been lying there, on pillows so soft they didn't even feel real. But it wasn't the pillows that mattered. My head was in someone's lap. His lap.

I remember my fingers in his hair—black, shining, spilling through my hand like I'd touched it a thousand times before. His eyes—Gods, those eyes—storm-dark blue, almost gray, like the sky right before it breaks open. They pinned me there, steady, familiar in a way that made my chest ache.

He looked... golden. Not in the "too many hours at the beach" way, but like the sun itself had claimed his skin. Perfect. Too perfect. Every time I tried to focus on his face, it blurred, slipped away like the dream was protecting him from me.

I don't even remember what he said. His voice was like static, like I should've known it, but couldn't tune it in. Didn't matter. The weight of it hit harder than the words could. He called me something though—Philinos? Philomenes? Some name that didn't belong to me, but somehow felt like it did.

Then he was gone. Just gone. Left me with jasmine in my lungs and the memory of fingers combing through hair I'd never touched.

And now here I was, parked outside the bar, chest tight like some delusional idiot with a crush on a dream. The vibration of my phone pulled me back to reality. I blinked, adjusting to the reality of the leather seat beneath me and the soft ticking of the car's dashboard.

A: Sorry I was asleep. What's up?

I had tried to call August after speaking with our mother the night before, after she'd told me about our father. How he had passed, and according to her, August had tried to reach me, but I had no record of any calls, no messages. Just silence.

S: Talked to Mom. She told me about Dad. How are you holding up?

I stared at the phone as the typing bubbles appeared, then disappeared, then reappeared at the bottom of the screen. Zayd was due any minute now, so I wouldn't have time to chat for long.

A: I tried to get ahold of you but you didn't answer. Sorry.

Another text quickly followed.

A: I'm fine.

I read those two words over and over. *I'm fine.* Empty. Like always. I wanted to push—ask if he actually gave a damn, if he even tried to call me, if Dad's death hit him at all. But my thumbs just hovered. That gap between us—years wide, crammed with missed calls and birthdays we didn't bother mentioning—it's too much. Too far. Too easy to just let it sit.

A soft knock on my window pulled me out of it. I looked up, and there he was—Zayd.

The morning sun lit him like some romance movie ad, sharp jawline framed in gold, dark hair falling into place like he had a personal stylist living in his closet. His smile warmed the air between us, and for a second I forgot about everything else. *Un angelo*, I thought automatically. An angel. And then immediately wanted to drive into the nearest tree for thinking it.

He was dressed neat, too neat—gray mock neck, black overcoat, pressed slacks. The kind of clean-cut that should've looked try-hard but didn't. It just...fit him.

I rolled down the window and gave him a smile I hoped passed for casual. "Morning. I can drive us, if you're ready."

The drive from Arroyo Grande to San Luis Obispo could've been awkward—two strangers in a car with nothing but the highway and the smell of my shitty air freshener between us. But it wasn't. The silence wasn't heavy, and when we did talk, it just... worked. Zayd had that kind of presence—easy, like the air after a storm. I hated how natural it felt.

The Mission rose ahead, white walls catching the sun like it hadn't aged a day in centuries. Cracks lined the plaster, but they weren't flaws—they were proof it had survived. Which, honestly, was more than I could say for me most days.

I shut the car door, gravel crunching underfoot, and gestured at the sprawling place like I was a tour guide who didn't get paid enough. "Here she is."

The sun stretched across the pillars, shadows falling in lazy stripes, like history was just napping here instead of buried. Zayd's gaze caught on everything—arches, stone, the geometry of old faith. He had this reverent stillness to him, like he was seeing something I couldn't. I wasn't used to quiet men, not the kind who made silence feel like it had weight.

"It's a beautiful spot," I said, giving him a sidelong look. "Why's it so important to you?"

He didn't answer right away. When he did, his voice was careful, low. "It's not for me. My employer has an interest. They want to keep it preserved. Untouched."

I raised a brow. "Your boss got a thing for old churches?"

A half-smile tugged at his mouth, gone before I could hold onto it. "They appreciate history. The beauty of what endures."

The way he said it made me pause. He wasn't just looking at the building—he was carrying something with it. Like every crack in the stone had carved itself into him. I found myself staring, caught between curiosity and something worse, something closer to wanting.

"Yeah," I muttered. "There's something to be said for what lasts." Even if people didn't.

We walked through the courtyard, our footsteps slow against the cobblestones. He touched the wall in passing, his fingers brushing it like he could pull the centuries into his palm. I didn't know why it unsettled me, but it did. Maybe because he looked like someone who actually belonged here—steady, timeless.

Inside, we stopped at a display case. Zayd's eyes locked on an old instrument—small, delicate, strings sagging like they'd given up centuries ago. But the air around it felt heavy, like music still lived in its bones.

He didn't move, just stared at it, jaw tight, expression unreadable. I leaned against the glass, arms crossed. "You look at this place like it's more than just a job."

He didn't answer right away. His fingers twitched, brushing the glass like he thought he could feel the history bleeding through it. When he finally spoke, his voice was quiet, almost reverent. "History is fragile," he said. "If we don't protect it, we lose it. And when we lose it, we lose the people who created it. The moments that made it real."

The words shouldn't have hit me the way they did, but something about them did. Maybe it was the way his mask slipped when he said it—the calm, put-together exterior cracking just enough for me to see what was underneath. And what was underneath wasn't just some guy doing his nine-to-five. Zayd actually *cared*.

Not in the shallow, cocktail-party way people pretend to care about history. No—he looked at this place like it was alive, like every crack in the stone mattered. It was the kind of sincerity you didn't see often, not in men our age, not in men at all, if I'm being honest. And fuck if it didn't make him even more distracting.

We moved on, our footsteps echoing in the museum's hush, the glass cases and faded photos like whispers of the people who came before us. It was strange, walking through time like that, realizing how much had burned away but how stubbornly the place itself stayed standing.

When we finally stepped back out, sunlight hit us full force, warm and blinding after all that cold air inside. I tilted my head back, squinting at the bell tower against the sky. "That's about it," I muttered, mostly to myself.

His eyes lingered on the Mission one last time, quiet admiration written all over him. And I found myself looking at him instead.

"Zayd," I said, stepping closer, close enough that I could catch the clean scent of his cologne, the kind that said effortless sophistication. The words tumbled out before I could stop them. "I'd like to see you again. Show you more places like this. There's a lot around here I think you'd like."

I didn't know why I said it. Hell, I didn't know why my chest felt tight, like I was about to ask him to move in instead of just coffee. But the thought of this ending here made my stomach knot.

His expression softened, just enough. Not shocked, not wary. Just... steady. Like he'd been expecting me to ask. "I'd like that," he said, voice smooth and polite. But there was something flickering underneath, a glint in his eyes that mirrored the restless thing gnawing at me.

My heart kicked up in my chest. *What the hell was this?* A stranger. And yet... there it was. Familiar. Like hearing a song you swear you know, but the lyrics stay just out of reach.

I forced a grin, needing to ground myself before I drowned in it. "We should probably exchange numbers."

He patted his jacket, then his pockets. Nothing. "I don't have my phone," he said finally, almost sheepish, though his mouth curved with the faintest smile. "You'll have to give me yours.

I barked out a laugh. "What, you a spy? A time traveler? Who doesn't have a phone?" I rattled off my number anyway, watching the way he nodded like he was carving it into his memory.

For a second, standing there, it almost felt like the future was holding its breath.

My apartment above the bar was quiet except for the hum of the old refrigerator and the occasional rattle of pipes. My bed creaked as I dropped onto it, staring at the ceiling like it might offer me answers. But all I could see was the Mission and Zayd.

I dragged a hand down my face, trying to shut my brain off, but the more I fought it, the heavier my thoughts grew, until sleep pulled me under.

And then I wasn't in Arroyo Grande anymore.

The air smelled of salt and incense, the mingling scents of a city by the sea. White stone buildings gleamed beneath the sun, their columns tall and proud, banners of crimson and gold fluttering high above the streets. I looked down and found myself draped in linen, a belt of leather cinching at my waist, sandals laced tight against my calves.

"Lykaios." The voice behind me was steady, rich with familiarity.

I turned, and there he was. The stranger from my other dream. His hair was darker here, long and pulled back with a thin band of gold. His eyes, though—storm-dark, bottomless—were the same. His features bore the sharpness of nobility, his bearing calm, assured. Even clothed in the simplicity of a traveler's tunic, he seemed untouchable, like he belonged to some higher realm.

I should've felt awe. Instead, there was warmth in my chest, the kind you only get from someone you've known forever.

"You'll be late," he said, lips quirking into the faintest smile.

I stepped closer without thinking, the worn stone cool beneath my sandals, the crowd around us blurring into insignificance. My hand brushed his arm, and it felt right—like it had a thousand times before, though I couldn't place when.

I didn't know his name, but I knew what he was to me. My lover. My mentor. My muse, even—the steady hand that had guided mine across parchment, the voice that had reminded me when words faltered that they could still sing.

"Lykaios," he repeated, the syllables curling from his lips like something sacred. He leaned down slightly, his eyes softening, his voice no louder than a whisper meant only for me.

We were late. The amphitheater waited. My words—our words—were set to take life in the mouths of actors, the swell of music, the heat of oil lamps. The city buzzed with expectation, eager to feast on art, on stories larger than themselves. And yet in that moment, with his gaze fixed on mine, the rest of the world blurred into insignificance.

"You cannot keep them waiting forever," he teased, but his hand brushed against mine, warm, grounding. He always did that—balanced discipline with gentleness, duty with desire. To others, he might have seemed a patron or a teacher. But to me? He was the reason ink still flowed when exhaustion hollowed me out. The reason the tragedies rose and the comedies bit with wit. The reason I believed my words could matter.

"Let them wait," I said, though my voice cracked under the weight of both nerves and affection. "It is nothing compared to a single breath from you."

His smile was faint but full, his thumb ghosting over the edge of my hand before he drew back. "Ever the dramatist," he murmured, and yet his eyes betrayed him, shining with the quiet pride of a man who knew the heart he inspired.

The marble pillars loomed ahead, banners stirring in the sea breeze. The sound of distant instruments tuning drifted through the air, carrying with it the heartbeat of the night to come. But all I could feel was him at my side, a constant—my anchor, my undoing, my salvation.

And so I did what I always did. Selfish I might have been, or perhaps simply enthralled. My hand slipped over his, and his eyes widened.

"Lykaios, people might see," he murmured, his gaze darting toward the others passing in the square.

But I said nothing. Instead, I tugged him toward the shadowed alley beside the theater, where crates were stacked high and the stone wall was cool against his back as I pressed him to it.

"Lykaios," he breathed again, the sound trembling as my hand slid up his chest, rising to cup the side of his face.

"Lykaios, Lykaios, Lykaios," I teased him with a crooked smile as I leaned close, my mouth brushing his just enough to taste the anticipation. "Starting to think that's all you know how to say."

His lips were soft, yielding, as they had been countless times before when he surrendered to my whims. His body bent toward mine, pliant with the ease of familiarity, with the weight of desire.

Then his hand rose, fingers tangling in my hair, and he pulled me in fully—closing the gap with a hungry urgency that swallowed us both whole.

I woke with a sharp breath, the darkness of the night pressing around me in my bedroom. My chest heaved, my pulse drumming like I'd run a mile. The dream clung to me, vivid and unshakable.

I raised my hand, brushing steady fingers over my lips. They still tingled, as though his kiss had been real. Too real.

And then the hardness between my legs reminded me of another truth. "...Fantastic," I muttered into the quiet. "Now I'm horny over some imaginary dream guy."

Chapter Five

Zayd

The wind of the Khaos moved with a strange quiet, a silence that seemed to stretch across centuries, thick as the shroud that separated us from the world of the mortals. Traveling to the old temple would be faster if I still had my wings—faster, more graceful. My fingers drifted absentmindedly to the place on my back where they had once been, feeling the fabric beneath them. The skin there was smooth, unmarked by the wings I had once taken for granted.

Once, I had soared through realms, traversed the world like a comet cutting through the dark. But now... now I was grounded, tethered to the earth like any other fallen thing. Eryx offered to fly me, but I refused. How could I accept such pity? To be carried like a broken thing, to cling to him as if I were something helpless? No. I already felt pathetic enough, stripped of everything that had once made me divine. Immortality was no blessing when all it left you with was a hollow shell, the ghost of what you once were. I couldn't cross into Aither or Erebos, couldn't touch the divine light nor the darkness of the Kakodaimon realm. I was... nothing. Nothing but a walking echo.

Eryx moved beside me, his steps barely making a sound in the thick fog of the Khaos. His presence was a burning contrast to the muted world around us, his energy thrumming with a vitality I couldn't understand anymore. I glanced at him, his features sharp and mischievous, as they always were—his gaze darting about with an amusement that never left him. How could he find joy in this void? But that was Eryx, wasn't it? He wore the world like a cloak, shifting its colors to suit his needs, his whims. Even now, his wings were hidden, tucked away somewhere beneath his many faces. He rarely let anyone see his true form anymore. Why bother, when you could be anything?

"Are you sure the Eudaimon will actually talk to me?" My voice sounded too small in the vastness of the Khaos.

"One of them owes me a favor," Eryx replied, his voice rich with that unshakable confidence, the kind that made it seem like he held the entire universe in his palm. "She doesn't have much of a choice."

I studied him for a moment, eyes narrowing. How was it that he could command such loyalty—or was it fear? How had he, a Kakodaimon, entangled an Eudaimon enough that she felt the need to honor a favor to him? *Was I missing something?* Some shift in the dynamics of the realm I'd been too lost in my misery to notice? Or was Eryx simply more clever than I gave him credit for? I had known him for so long, kept his company, and yet... what did I really know of his dealings, of the tasks the Theion had set for him? All I knew was that he thrived in the shadows of human greed and lust, his hands in the wealth of the corrupt.

"Eryx," I began slowly, my voice lowering. "Have you ever seen a tattoo—a dagger with a Celtic cross as the hilt?"

He stopped for a moment, his gray eyes flickering with surprise, the scar through his brow lifting one side higher than the other. "Callaghan," he murmured, the word weighted with history. "An old mafia family. Irish roots before they set up in California. Drugs, arms dealing—the usual." His voice shifted, eyes narrowing. "Is that who came for Silas?"

I nodded, my heart tightening with the weight of it.

Eryx's expression darkened for a moment, then lightened just as quickly. "Your human should be careful. He's been out of the game for too long. The Callaghans, they've been under fire recently. Someone betrayed them, and now they're scrambling. Bad for business, but good for their enemies like—"

I didn't need him to finish. The name fell from my lips like a curse. "Legare."

"Bingo."

We fell into silence again, but my mind was racing. What if Silas' soul tie had snapped because it wasn't a second chance at all? What if it was a warning? What if his death was near, and this time it would come at the hands of the Callaghans?

He had pulled away from his family, from the blood and violence that had birthed him. For a while, I thought he might have a chance at peace. But no one escapes their past, do they? I could only intervene so much. If the threads of fate were drawing tight around his neck, there was little I could do to loosen them.

The temple loomed ahead, its worn stone steps rising from the mists like bones from an ancient grave. "The Temple of Kyrova," Eryx said, his voice breaking the stillness as we reached the crumbling edifice. It had seen better days, the wear of millennia marking every crack, every vine that curled around its pillars. The gods were no longer worshiped as they once were—mortals had forgotten their names, their power. The Theion were distant now, their tools, the Daimons, all that remained of their touch. But the temple still stood, an echo of the old ways, its walls whispering of forgotten traditions and stories.

We stepped out of Khaos to join the figure that awaited us inside, a woman it seemed. But I knew better. No mere mortal woman could possess such beauty—her chestnut skin glowed in the dim light, her obsidian curls framing her face with a grace that was both regal and untouchable. Her wings, large and white as a dove's, rested behind her, and her fingers traced the ancient etchings in the stone as if reading the stories of gods long gone.

"Malaika," Eryx greeted her, his voice slipping over her name like honey, familiar and intimate.

She looked up, her eyes a mesmerizing blend of green and brown, the gaze of one who had seen far too much, and yet, still remained above it all.

"So this is the forsaken," Malaika purred, her voice curling through the cold air like smoke, each syllable deliberate, laced with the richness of centuries. Her words were not a question but a statement, as if carved in stone. Her eyes flicked over me, assessing, but there was no warmth there, no recognition beyond the surface. "I see that having your wings clipped did not take away your beauty, brother."

I scoffed, the bitterness rising before I could swallow it down. "As if we are family," I spat, the words slipping out with more venom than I intended. But I couldn't hold it back, not after all this time. "Not one of you saved me. Not one of you even thought to offer release, or comfort, or anything beyond cold indifference. A Kako-" I hesitated, the edge of my tongue sharp with something unspoken. I would not—could not—direct my scorn at Eryx. Despite everything, for all his faults, the fact that he was a Kakodaimon, he had came, and he had stayed.

The Eudaimon had forsaken me just as the Theion had. Once, they would have embraced me as one of their own, but now they avoided me, as if even acknowledging my presence might taint them, might drag them into the same darkness where I was cast.

The Kakodaimon kept their distance too, but it was not pity or avoidance of divine retribution that held them back. No, they feared Eryx, his power a quiet warning, a shadow that followed me wherever I went. None would approach me—not while he was at my side, not even in his absence. They knew better.

"Once the lance of the Theion has been thrown, we may not intervene. You should know this, Zayd." Her voice caressed my name, twisting it into something unrecognizable. I hated the sound of it on her lips, hated how easily she spoke as if the centuries of my torment were nothing but a passing moment.

Eryx's hand landed on my shoulder, his grip firm, grounding. "My apologies, Malaika," he said with a chuckle that held no real mirth. "Zayd's had a rough few... well, centuries." His tone was casual, too light for the weight of the moment, and yet it fit him—always dancing on the edge of something heavier, something unspoken. "He seeks an audience with the Theion. Can you make that happen?"

Malaika paused, her gaze sliding over me like a blade, sharp, lingering. She perched herself on the stone table at the temple's center, her movements languid, feline. "One does not simply request an audience with the Theion," she said, stretching her limbs as if to emphasize the impossibility of the notion. Her wings unfurled slightly, a shimmer of white against the darkening air, a reminder of the divinity I had lost.

Eryx, ever undeterred, pressed on. "So you're saying it's not possible?"

"Mm, that is not what I said," she murmured, crossing her legs with an elegance that was almost maddening, her hands resting delicately on her knee. "It is rare, yes, but not unheard of. Mortals have sought their counsel before, and the Theion, in their infinite wisdom, have been known to humor them."

I felt the irritation coil inside me, tight and hot. "But I am not a mortal," I growled, my brow furrowing as the weight of her game settled in. She was toying with us, dragging this out for her own amusement, or perhaps to remind us both of my diminished standing. She was wasting time, and time was a luxury neither of us could afford. The Eudaimon weren't even allowed in the mortal realm anymore. We were bound to influence from the shadows, hidden from the mortal eye. Whatever risk she thought she was avoiding, it was her own.

"No, you're not," she said, her voice soft, infuriatingly calm. "But you have a mortal, don't you? Get him to make the offering, perform the ritual, and beg for an audience." Her smile was knowing, as if she thought it the simplest thing in the world, as if I would drag Silas into this chaos without a second thought.

"I'm not getting Silas involved," I said, the words a quiet vow, more to myself than to her.

"Silas," she echoed, her voice wrapping around the name, tasting it. "*Prayed for.* How fitting." Her gaze flickered to the ancient carvings etched into the temple walls, the remnants of long-forgotten traditions. "The ritual is here, engraved in stone, should you become desperate enough."

"I won't." The words came out as a sigh, my hand running over the back of my neck. My eyes traced the old symbols on the walls.

"What is it you seek, Zayd?" Her voice had softened, curiosity creeping in as she stepped down, closing the space between us. I could feel her studying me, her eyes probing the empty place where my wings had once been, searching for something—weakness, perhaps. Or maybe she simply wanted to see the wreckage up close.

"Silas... Philetos," I began, the names now tasting foreign on my tongue, one anchored in the present, the other lost to history. "Our soul tie has snapped. Prematurely. He still lives, but his presence... it's gone." The weight of that absence pressed against my chest, a hollow ache where once there had been the steady beat of two hearts entwined. Now, there was only mine.

Her gaze flickered with something I couldn't place, a glimmer of emotion quickly buried beneath layers of stoic control. She glanced toward Eryx, whose expression remained unreadable. "I am a Daimon of my word," she said at last, her tone shifting to something almost reverent. "I have not yet fulfilled my part of our bargain—Eryx remains unsatisfied. I will speak with the others, consult with those who dwell closer to the Theion, and bring back whatever knowledge I uncover."

Eryx turned to me then, his eyes searching. "Would that work for you, Zayd?"

"Yes," I said, my voice steady, though inside, doubt still gnawed at the edges of my thoughts. I turned to Malaika, meeting her gaze. "Yes, that works for me."

She nodded, her form already beginning to fade into the shadows. "Then we will be in touch. Eryx... Zayd." Her voice lingered in the air, even as her presence slipped away, leaving only the echo of her parting words.

As soon as she was gone, Eryx let out a soft laugh. "Now we just have to wait. That shouldn't be hard for you."

I wanted to laugh, but all I felt was the gnawing uncertainty inside me. "No," I replied, my voice barely more than a whisper. "It shouldn't be." But it would be—waiting was always the hardest part. Every moment without an answer was a moment closer to losing everything.

Chapter Six

Silas

My phone buzzed in my pocket, a soft pulse against the silence of the study. I pulled it out, and there it was on the screen: It's Zayd.

I let out a breath I didn't realize I'd been holding, my chest unclenching just a little. Days of silence, and I'd started convincing myself I'd imagined the whole connection—that maybe I'd come on too strong, or worse, that I'd bored him. Pathetic. Grown man, Legare's heir, bartender, take your pick—and here I was grinning at my phone like a teenager who'd just been noticed.

Before I could type back, my mother's voice broke through. "Are you staying for supper? Augustus should be home by then."

Her heels tapped softly on the worn wood as she moved, each step a ghost of the authority she once wielded with ease. She sank into my father's old chair—the big, ornate one that had always looked more like a throne. It swallowed her now. She looked smaller, frailer, already draped in black like she'd been rehearsing widowhood long before Cesare finally keeled over.

"I'll try to make it," I said, pocketing my phone with a quick glance to the message I hadn't yet answered. "There are a few things I need to take care of tonight."

The table between us was cluttered with photographs—snapshots of a family we'd never really been. I picked one up, the edges soft, the gloss worn thin. There we were, the four of us, posed stiffly for one of our annual family portraits. August, barely seven, his face round with baby fat still, and me at thirteen, already trying to play the role of eldest son. To anyone outside these walls, we would have looked like the perfect family—Cesare Vassallo, the towering patriarch, with his wife and sons by his side.

But I remembered. The makeup my mother had carefully pressed into my skin to cover the bruise around my eye. The reprimand I had received for some minor disobedience. Appearances were everything to him.

I put the photograph back down with a soft exhale, a thousand unsaid things swelling in my throat. Cesare Vassallo. King of Legare. Believer in money, loyalty, and the occasional backhand. And now? Dead. Did anyone truly miss him? My mother mourned him, yes, but was it grief for the man or for the chains that would soon fall on her sons?

I stood, casting a last look at the photographs—the scripted memories, the lies frozen in time.

"Ma," I said, and her eyes, so much like my own, flickered up to meet mine. "I have to head out but I'll try to make it for supper... Don't torture yourself with those pictures too long. You only need five for the memorial."

Her lips quirked, but it was the sort of smile that carried more weariness than warmth. "*Ti voglio bene.*"

"I love you too." I leaned down, pressing a soft kiss to her head, breathing in the faint scent of her perfume—rose-oud and amber-vanilla.

Stepping into the hallway, I caught a glimpse of a figure as familiar as the scent of varnished wood and polished marble clinging to these walls. "Arnaldo," I greeted, voice light, smile already tugging at my lips. "Told you I'd come home."

"You did not tell me that." His reply was low, gruff, and so thoroughly Arnaldo it could've been carved in stone. Broad-shouldered, immaculate as always, he looked like age had barely bothered with him. Sharp suit, sharper eyes. My father's right hand—his shadow, his blade, his Sottocapo. And now, with Cesare dead, he was the one holding the leash until the dogs decided which Vassallo son would take the throne. For now, Arnaldo was king.

"I didn't?" I chuckled, stepping in to clasp his shoulder. The solidity of him under my hand was oddly grounding, even if his face gave me nothing in return. "Must be getting old. Your memory's slipping." Half-joke, half-truth, but threaded with warmth. "Good seeing you again, old friend. Thanks for looking after my mother and August."

The stare he leveled at me was the same one I'd grown up with—like he was waiting for the punchline, waiting for me to stop pretending I had a heart.

And then the words slipped out before I could stop them. "Do me a favor, would you? For old times' sake."

He didn't answer. Just kept looking at me with those dark, heavy eyes that could strip a man down to the bone. No refusal, though, which was something. So I pushed, leaning on charm like it was armor.

"I need you to look into someone. Potential business partner." My tone was easy, but we both knew nothing about this was casual. "His name's Zayd. Works for some investor tied to the South County Historical Society. Old mission in San Luis Obispo. My age, maybe late twenties, early thirties."

Arnaldo turned fully now, crossing his arms in that stance I knew too well. The same stance he'd take when I screwed up in front of my father, the one that said *you're an idiot and I'm watching you prove it.*

"No last name?" His voice cut sharp. He let the silence stretch, like he wanted me to feel just how stupid he thought I sounded. And when I didn't bite, he twisted the knife. "You're potentially doing business with a man you don't even have a last name for?"

I shrugged, unbothered. "Think of it as a challenge. See if you and your men still know how to do your jobs."

For a long moment, he just stared at me, stone-faced. Then finally, with all the enthusiasm of a man agreeing to take out the trash, he said: "I will see what I can find."

Flat. Cold. But it was still a promise. And that was all I needed.

The warehouse smelled like copper and gun oil. Shadows clung to the rafters, heavy as the silence that always comes after the violence is done. I'd moved like I'd been taught—quiet, efficient, no wasted motion. Three men down, one left breathing. The Callaghans had always been stubborn, but tonight they were something worse: unprepared.

He'd been the unlucky one. The one I decided to keep. He sat slumped in the chair I'd tied him to, his face a mask of blood and sweat, lips split but sealed tight. Stubborn bastard. I'd broken fingers, dislocated a shoulder, pressed a blade where it mattered, but he gave me nothing. Not a name, not a plan, not even a bluff worth spitting back at me.

It was textbook Legare—my father's style. The kind of "clean work" he'd applauded when I was young, when he'd still pretended I was his heir and not just another tool. And here I was, slipping back into it like an old coat.

By the time I put the gun to his temple, my hands weren't even shaking. He spat at my shoes. I pulled the trigger. Quick. Efficient. Another ghost for the pile.

I raised the cigarette to my lips, the paper thin and brittle against my skin. The flame caught with a soft crackle, trembling at the tip before settling into a steady burn. I dragged slow, deliberate, the heat sinking deep into my lungs until it ached. For a moment, the world blurred at the edges—just me, the smoke, and the silence. Then I exhaled, watching the gray curl upward before the night swallowed it whole, gone like everything else I try to leave behind.

I told myself I was done with this. Done with all of it. But here I was anyway, standing in the back alley of some godforsaken building, the air thick with blood and regret. My hand raked through my hair before my head thudded against the wall behind me. Cold brick against my skull—grounding, if not exactly comforting. "What the hell am I doing?" The words slipped out quiet, carried off like the smoke.

I could justify it. Easy. They threatened me, threatened my family. They came at me with guns drawn. I needed answers; they weren't going to give them up for free. That's the clean version, the one my father would have approved of without blinking. But the truth? The truth is uglier. I liked it. The hit of adrenaline when my fist connected. The sharp thrill when the gun went off. I can dress it up as necessity all I want, but deep down I know—I didn't hate it. Not the violence. Not the blood. What I hated was the interruption. The fact that I had to crawl back into this at all.

Am I selfish? A psychopath? Both?

The thought gnawed at me until I lit another drag, pulling hard, burning fast. The ember flared bright before I let it drop to the ground and crushed it under my heel. Snuffed out in an instant. Just like that.

I wanted out. Still do. But the worst part? I know how well I fit into Legare. Like a suit tailored to me before I was old enough to choose my own damn clothes. Peace without blood, without the weight of expectation—that's what I wanted. That's what I told myself, anyway.

And yet... maybe it'd be easier just to come back.

My phone buzzed in my pocket, dragging me out of my thoughts and back into the cold, damp reality of the alley. I answered without looking, lifting it to my ear.

"The man you wanted me to look into..." Arnaldo's voice was low, rough as ever. "I'm not finding anything on him."

I froze, letting the silence stretch for a beat. Nothing? Not even a breadcrumb? The name had to be fake, but Zayd hadn't struck me as the type to hand out lies so easily. Then again, nothing about him had sat neatly since the moment he walked into my bar. He was off—different. I just couldn't tell if my instincts were warning me or leading me by the nose.

"One more thing," Arnaldo added, his voice like gravel over stone. "The South County Historical Society... no significant donors, no one with any special interest in the mission in San Luis Obispo."

I bit back a grin, the corner of my lips twitched with the realization. *Of course.* "Thank you, Arnaldo," I said, my voice even, though there was a flicker of something darker beneath it. "Seems you haven't lost your edge. Very timely." But before I could say more, the line goes dead, leaving me in silence once again.

I lowered the phone, staring out at the empty street beyond the alley, the city sprawling and indifferent, unaware of the games being played in its shadows. *Am I being played?* The thought turned over in my mind, sharp as glass. Zayd arrived at the same time as the Callaghans, didn't he? Like a Trojan horse, dressed up as my savior, slipping into my life with his easy charm and perfect timing.

And now... now I wondered if he'd been a part of their plan all along.

"I'm sorry I'm late," I said as I stepped into the dining room, the comforting scent of rosemary and garlic wrapped around me like an old, worn blanket. My fingers were busy with the cuffs of my shirt, unbuttoning them, rolling the fabric up as if shedding the weight of the day would somehow bring me relief. My gaze drifted, distracted by the small ritual, until his voice sliced through the air.

"I was just leaving."

I looked up. There, beside my mother, sat August—grown beyond the boy I left behind at nineteen. His face, chiseled now, carries the unmistakable features of our father. The same hair, thick and dark, the same eyes—brown so deep they swallowed whatever light tried to touch them. For a second, it was like looking backward and forward at once. When the hell had he grown up?

"*Cucciolo*," my mother's voice, soft yet edged with that sadness I recognize all too well. "Your brother just got here. Please, stay a bit longer."

August sighed, a sound heavy with the weight of our history, and even though I could see the resistance in the set of his shoulders, I knew he'd stay. Neither of us could ever bring ourselves to disappoint her, no matter the storm that brewed between us. He sat back down, his movement slow, reluctant, and I followed suit, pulling out the chair across from him. My mother sat between us, like some fragile bridge over a chasm neither of us were willing to cross.

"You need to eat," she said, her voice gentle as her fingers brushed over my forearm, tracing the veins like rivers, seeking something beneath. Her hand slipped into mine, holding it as though I might slip away at any moment. "You're looking thin. I'll call Luisel to get you a plate." She turned to August, repeating the gesture, connecting us both in her quiet, steady way.

"No, that's alright," I lied, my stomach churning with something far too bitter to be hunger. "I'm not hungry. I had a big lunch earlier." Truth is, I felt sick. Sick with anger, with something festering beneath my skin that I can't quite name.

"Work make you lose your appetite?" August muttered, low, almost to himself. His eyes flicked to my sleeve, catching on the faint dark specks that saturated through the rolled up fabric. Judgment. Always there, quiet but sharp. He took a sip of whatever he was drinking, let it sit like punctuation.

"Nosebleed," I said with a crooked smile, tapping the fabric. "Ruins every good shirt."

It was flimsy, but I've never needed him to believe me. His judgment's been there since the first time he saw me for what I was. He was nine. I was fifteen. Our father put a gun in my hand and told me to use it. I didn't hesitate. I didn't regret it. August watched me then, and something between us broke. Years later, when it was his turn, he cried. I didn't. That was the difference. That's when he decided I was the monster.

"You still get those? At your age?" My mother's worry was like a thin veil, transparent and ever-present. Her fingers moved to trace the tattoo on my hand, a gesture so familiar, so maternal, that my little lies almost broke me. "Have you seen a doctor?"

"It doesn't happen often, mamma," My voice softened, giving her the smile I knew she needed to see. "Nothing to worry about."

She returned the smile, but it didn't quite reach her eyes. "How are you, August?" I turned to him, desperate to shift the weight of her attention. "Are you still in college, or did you graduate?"

Her answer came before he could even open his mouth. "He pulled out five years ago."

August cut her off, the bitterness sharp in his voice, though it was not directed towards her. "I didn't pull out. Father forced me to quit. Said it was a waste of time." His eyes, full of scorn, fell to the table, refusing to meet mine.

"Father's dead now," I reminded him, leaning forward, my words a subtle offer. "You can always go back."

"I can't—" His glass hit the table, the sound too loud, too final. He slipped his hand free from our mother's grasp, rising from his seat. "I can't pretend you didn't abandon us... Abandon me." The words hit like stones, heavy and cruel. He stood there, towering over us both, tears swelling in his eyes, but not falling, not yet.

"Augustus, please," our mother whispered, her hand stretched toward him, but fell short.

"You left us with that monster," he said, voice breaking as he gestured to me, to the blood-stained sleeve that marks me as everything he despised "For what? To play at being normal? I could understand if you actually pulled it off, but clearly, you didn't." His eyes burned into mine, and I felt the weight of it, the fury, the grief, everything he'd carried all these years. And then, just as quickly, he turned away.

"August, I—" The words caught in my throat as he walked out, the heavy wooden doors slammed shut behind him, echoing in the silence.

I moved to stand, to follow, but my mother's grip tightened on my hand. "Let him be," she said, her voice like a balm, soft and soothing. "He's been through a lot, *tesoro mio.*"

I sank back into the chair, my breath shaky as it escaped me. "Do you... do you feel I abandoned you too?" The question is out before I could stop it, hanging in the air between us, fragile and uncertain.

Her eyes softened, and a smile, warm and tender, pulled at her lips. "Silas, you're too precious. I am your mother. I can take care of myself." Her hand moved to my face, cupping my cheek, her thumb brushed gently over my skin as though she could wipe away the years of distance, of guilt. "You did not abandon me. I promise."

But she didn't say *us*. And that silence spoke louder than her smile.

I kissed the back of her hand, pressing my apology there because I couldn't say it out loud. "I have to go. But I'll be back soon." Thin words, stretched too far. But they were all I had.

Perhaps I should've slowed down. Paced myself. But patience was never my strong suit, and the thoughts kept rattling around in my head like loose change in a jar. The vodka dulled it, sure, but not enough. Never enough.

"I'll take another," I said, pushing the empty glass forward with two fingers. Then, after a beat, "Actually—make it two."

The bartender hesitated, his hand hovering over the bottle. "Alright, sir. But after these, I'll have to cut you off."

I leaned across the counter, voice dropping, my smile a shade too sharp. "Cut me off? That's cruel. You'd do that to me?" I let my gaze travel over him, deliberately slow—his throat, the line of his jaw, the way his lips pressed together like he didn't trust them to stay still. "Tell you what... you keep pouring, and I'll make it worth your while."

His ears went pink first, then the blush crawled down his neck. He tried to look away, but he didn't. His hand trembled faintly as he poured, the liquor sloshing before he steadied it. I didn't miss the way his eyes flicked down to my mouth when I smirked at him.

"You've got a good mouth," I said casually, as though complimenting the drink. The words landed heavy, deliberate. His throat bobbed as he swallowed, his fingers tightening around the bottle.

"Sir—" he started, but his voice cracked, betraying him.

"Don't call me sir," I cut in, my tone low, suggestive. "Makes it sound like I'm paying you for more than drinks."

He laughed, nervous, embarrassed, but there was a glint in his eyes that said he wasn't opposed. When he set the shots down in front of me, our fingers brushed—he didn't pull away, and neither did I.

Somewhere between the fifth shot and the way he kept stealing glances at me, the night tipped over the edge. He muttered something about "taking this outside," and I let him lead me through the staff door, the two of us cutting into the cold air.

Next thing I knew, I was against my car, his hands tugging at my belt, my own fist tangled in his hair as his mouth wrapped around me. He was eager, sloppy in a way that was almost charming, the heat of him sharp against the chill of the night. My breath stuttered, a low groan slipping out as my head tipped back, lips parting to the cold sky.

He tried to make it good for me—I could feel it in every desperate pull of his mouth, the way he moaned like he needed me to hear it. And it should've been enough. Should've been more than enough.

But my thoughts were elsewhere.

Zayd.

Even with another man's lips wrapped around my dick, another man's tongue trying to wring a reaction from me, I couldn't get his face out of my head. The sharp cut of his jaw. The blue of his eyes—so deep they almost hurt to look at. *Who the fuck are you, Zayd?* Why do you feel like need, like something I can't drink or fuck my way out of?

The pressure coiled low, insistent, but it never broke. My body refused, like some locked door I couldn't kick down.

I pulled away from him, abrupt. His lips were swollen, wet, his eyes confused, almost pleading. "Did I... did I do something wrong?" he asked, voice small, pathetic in its eagerness.

But I didn't see him. I couldn't. All I saw were those ocean eyes staring back at me, drowning me.

Would I be an asshole if I called him? Sent some sloppy drunk text, just to see if my theory was right—that I couldn't fuck him away. That no amount of bodies, no amount of mouths or hands, would cut him out of me. But that would open a different can of worms... because if I got him, would I even be able to let him go?

And then there was the other thing. That beautiful fucker lied to me.

I sighed, tucking myself back in, zipping up, buckling my belt like I hadn't just let some stranger on his knees try to replace a ghost. My fingers dragged through my hair, my chest still tight.

Do I even care that he lied? I don't know. I don't know if that scares me more... or that I just want him.

My head tipped back, eyes closed, the pulse in my chest hammering louder than the city around me. All I could hear was his name, beating in time with my heart.

Zayd.

Chapter Seven

Zayd

He was drunk—undeniably, irretrievably lost to the liquor. He swayed like a reed caught in a storm. I should have been relieved that at least he had the sense not to drive, though the thought that I would've had to step in if he had was a cold, bitter reminder of the fragility of mortals.

It took all the restraint in me to stand back, silent, while some stranger stood pressed against him in the dimness of the night, their hands tangled in a frenzy of desperation. I watched, breath held, as Silas surrendered to his impulses, with no thought for consequence or meaning, as though it was nothing. And yet, it wasn't enough for him. I am nothing more than a stranger to him, and he called, I came. Am I nothing more than another stranger to fall back on when his indulgence wears thin? I know I had no right to feel these feelings, jealousy and anger but it festered in me.

Silas' appearance was different, like an echo of himself from before he left Legare. Blond hair pushed back with deliberate care, a few rogue strands were left to fall artfully across his brow. He was draped in a crisp white shirt with the sleeves rolled up, a black tie that whispered of formality, and shoes that gleamed like polished obsidian, as expensive as the glinting watch that circled his wrist. It was the opposite of his small-town bartender charm, the way he plays at humility, effortlessly slipping between roles like changing masks for a masquerade.

I finally approached him, leaving the Khaos as he was lounging against the sleek body of his car. It was the kind of vehicle that turned heads and left a trail of envy in its wake—a stark contrast to the vehicle he had driven me in days ago. His arms were folded across his chest, head tipped back as if the world itself had bored him. Even drunk, he held himself with a casual grace that made my own restraint feel like a burden.

"Silas." My voice was quiet as I approached, uncertain how to navigate this encounter. Years I've watched him, studied him, and yet still, he was unpredictable, like the ocean—beautiful, deadly, and ungraspable.

His eyes fluttered open, lids heavy with intoxication, and he regarded me with a lazy smile that didn't reach his eyes. "Zayd." The way he said my name, smooth as silk, almost made me forget how careless he'd been tonight. "Didn't mean to drag you out here, but... I thought maybe we could hang out. Grab a drink together." He stepped forward, his gait unsteady, the weight of the alcohol made him stumble.

"Silas," I sighed, closing the distance between us, my hands found the solid warmth of his sides, as I gently pressed him back against the car. He was so close now, too close, and it took everything in me to keep my composure. "You're drunk." The words were a soft reprimand, though there was no real bite to them. "I don't think you should have another drink. Is there someone I can call to take you home?"

The warmth of his breath fanned against my skin, tinged with the sharp scent of liquor and tobacco. His hands found my hips, pulling me toward him, and I inhaled sharply. I wasn't expecting that.

"No one else... I called you, didn't I? And you came. Right? No need for anyone else to get me." His words slurred slightly, the alcohol loosening his tongue, but there was a weight to them that lingered, that hooked into me.

"Which is it? Would you like a ride? Or to hang out?" I replied, trying to pull back, but his grip tightened, anchoring me to him. I felt the warmth of him, his breath brushed against my neck, and the air between us seemed to thicken. "Is there somewhere I can take you to rest?"

"Zayd," he murmured again, his voice softening, almost reverent. His hands were slow, deliberate as they trailed up my back, one rested just below my shoulder blades, the other settled at the small of my back. "Zayd." He said it again, and that time, my name sounded like something precious in his mouth; it felt like home. I watched his lips, plush and soft, before my gaze met his, heavy with intent.

He leant in, slow and deliberate, as though the moment between us was fragile, and then his lips brushed mine, like a spark catching flame. He pulled away just enough for us to breathe, the air between us charged with something raw, something dangerous. It lasted only a heartbeat, but it stretched, infinite in its intensity.

And then I closed the distance, my lips crashed against his, the weight of centuries—lifetimes— pressed into the kiss, and he met me with a hunger that felt like it could swallow me whole. My hand found its way to the back of his head, fingers tangling in his hair, and I tasted the sharp, bitter tang of liquor on his tongue as it slid against mine.

I was losing myself, losing all sense of restraint, caught in a whirlpool of emotion and memory, the flood of all the things I've held back for so long. His lips trailed down my neck, and I groaned, low and guttural, as I felt his arousal hard against my hip. I shifted, pressing into him, and he breathed a sharp needy sound that pulled me deeper into the moment.

"Is Zayd your real name?" His breath was warm against my skin, sending shivers down my spine. "I want to make sure I moan the right name." There was something almost wicked in the way he said it, the way his words brushed against the cool night air.

I froze, just for a moment, before I remembered to breathe. "Yes." The word slipped out on a breath, barely audible.

"Then why can't my people find you?" He asked, as he pressed his lips to the sensitive skin of my neck, and I felt the weight of his question settle in the back of my mind.

"Running a background check on me?" I tried for nonchalance, though I knew exactly what he'd been doing. I was there, spectating from the Khaos when he asked his father's lackey to dig into my past. I knew he would not find anything, as I am no one, at least not to the mortals. But Eryx helped with that—crafted a history for me. The next time someone checks, a false life will be attached to my name; connecting to some wealthy history buff from Massachusetts who donates to nonprofits in Southern California.

"Give me your last name," he said, his voice a low rumble as his tongue flicked against my skin.

"Aristodemos." It was the first name that came to mind when Eryx wove my false identity, the name of Philetos' father from so long ago.

"Aristodemos?" He chuckled lazily, his breath warm against my neck. "I wouldn't have guessed that."

"What? Don't like it?" I asked, my voice soft, vulnerable in a way I hadn't intended.

"It suits you," he said, and though he didn't know it, those words made my heart stutter.

His head dropped against my chest, and I ran my fingers through his hair, the gesture instinctive, comforting. "I'm sorry," he muttered, a weight in his words that had nothing to do with the alcohol.

"There's nothing to apologize for," I murmured, my hand stilled for a moment before resuming its slow, soothing rhythm.

"But there is," he insisted, his voice slurred but sincere. "I don't have to be sober to know I've messed things up."

I paused once more, then continued, my fingers tracing idle paths through his hair. "If I didn't want to be here, Silas, I wouldn't be. There's nowhere else I'd rather be." It was the truth, even if I don't fully understand why he's being drawn to me so soon. Perhaps it was the remnants of our bond, or perhaps it was something more. All I knew was I've waited centuries for this moment, and I don't care what brought it about—only that it's finally here.

"Can you take me to a hotel?" he asked, his voice quiet, almost boyish. "I don't trust myself to drive, and I don't want to disrespect my mother by showing up like this."

"Of course," I replied, my voice soft, filled with everything I cannot yet say.

He was barely clothed, only the low-hanging fabric of his pants clinging to his hips as I guided him toward the bed, his steps unsteady, a heavy grace in the way he moved, like a lion lulled by fatigue. My eyes could not help but linger on the landscape of his body, the sinew beneath skin pulled taut and smooth over muscles that had known violence, and yet, here they were, softened, surrendering to exhaustion. His body—beautiful, yes, something carved and weathered into shape—but also a canvas of his life, a tale etched in scars, each mark a punctuation in the history of fights fought and perhaps lost, fights ignited by the same fiery impulse that now simmered in the liquor-flushed hue of his skin.

His tattoos were a mosaic, a patchwork of stories drawn across his flesh. On his left arm, there were the marks of his heritage—Roman columns rising like pillars of antiquity, olive branches curling in delicate, endless loops, a tribute to a history long written in the blood of kings and legions. And then, as though to break the solemnity, a ridiculous caricature of pasta, absurd and out of place, yet so distinctly him—a testament to his bold, blunt charm, the ability to mock the very things that defined him. His hand bore another tale, a skull inked in sharp relief, a rose entwined beneath it, and a moth poised on its crown—a reminder, perhaps, of the fragility of life, or the strange dance between death and beauty.

His back, emblazoned between his shoulder blades, was the symbol of his family, the indelible mark of Legare: an ouroboros, the serpent devouring its own tail, the cycle unbroken, eternal, framed by a laurel wreath, the symbol of victory and honor in a lineage built on ruthless ambition. Above it, the words "*Fedele fino alla Morte*"—loyal until death.

He sank into the mattress, the muscles rippling across his back in one final act of defiance against the exhaustion that threatened to claim him. I stood there, momentarily suspended between action and thought, watching as the blanket draped over him like a shroud. I was ready to leave, to retreat back to the safety of the shadows, but then his hand caught my wrist, a silent plea in the gesture, the sleepiness in his voice pulling me back.

"Zayd," he murmured, his voice a warm breath of sound that stirred the space between us. "Lay with me."

And there it was—that flicker of vulnerability that unmade me. I had never been able to resist him, not in this life nor in the ones before it. How could I prefer to watch him from the distant cold of Khaos when he asked me to be here, with him, in this fleeting warmth?

"Okay," I breathed, the word small, almost broken, but it was all I could manage.

I slipped off my jacket, then my shoes, casting them aside with little thought, my body moving of its own accord. As I slid under the covers beside him, the heat of his skin radiated toward me even though we didn't yet touch. The anticipation hummed in the space between us. I waited, not long, for him to move closer, his arm sliding around my waist, pulling me toward him. His head found its place on my chest, his breath warm and steady, the weight of him grounding me in this moment that felt both surreal and yet inevitable.

"Thank you," he whispered, his voice a slurred prayer of gratitude as he drifted off, surrendering to the weight of sleep.

I reached out to switch off the lamp, the room dissolving into the gentle darkness that was only punctuated by the faint glow of city lights slipping through the sheer curtains. The world outside seemed so far away now, distant and unimportant, as though it had shrunk to this—just the two of us, the quiet, and the slow rhythm of his breathing, the anchor that kept me tethered to the present.

My hand drifted to rest on his shoulder, the other moving to trace idle patterns on his forearm. Daimons did not need sleep. We lived beyond it, immune to the calls of fatigue, but there, in that moment, wrapped in his warmth, I felt the pull of it, the exhaustion not of the body but of centuries of waiting, of longing, finally softened by the press of his skin against mine. And so, in that rarest of moments, I closed my eyes, allowing myself to drift alongside him, into whatever peace his presence could offer me.

Chapter Eight

Silas

The dream didn't come gently. It slid in like smoke under a door, curling around me, pulling me into someplace that wasn't mine. I wasn't myself—at least, not the version I knew. I was inside someone else, caught in their skin, their heartbeat echoing through me like a second pulse. A woman this time.

She sat on a porch that sagged with age, boards creaking under the steady rhythm of her rocking chair. The kind of place you'd find rotting out in the middle of nowhere. Her hands moved slow, practiced, a needle flashing in and out of fabric, pulling a flower into being stitch by stitch. Her voice hummed some old tune, low and warm, like honey poured slow from the jar.

Then the boards groaned again—heavier, sharper. Boots. A shadow stretched long across the porch, and I felt her—felt me—look up.

And there he was.

Tall. Broad shoulders filling the space. Coat worn from the road, hair tied back loose with strands slipping free. The kind of face you don't forget even if you want to, sharp enough to cut the light. And those eyes. My chest clenched with the certainty before my head could catch up.

It was him. Just like the man from the other dreams, the one whose face I could never quite reach. Until now.

"Zayd," I whispered, the name soft as breath, slipping past my lips before I even thought it. My heart leapt, aching, full. "My love... I missed you." The words broke something in me, something that had been wound tight in his absence. My voice carried the ache of weeks without him.

He stepped close, knelt before me, the boards creaking under his weight. His hand found mine, warm, rough from travel, steadying me as though I had been drifting without him. I let the needle fall, the fabric slipping forgotten into my lap as I clutched his hand like it was the only thing that tethered me to the earth.

"You shouldn't have come," I said, though the words faltered, weak against the truth beating in my chest.

"You knew I would." His voice sank deep into me, low and certain, each syllable a vow. His thumb brushed over my knuckles, and I leaned into it, desperate for his touch. "I always do, Evangeline." He whispered as his lips brushed my cheek, gentle, reverent, and I closed my eyes, the world around us fading until there was only him, his hand, his breath, his presence.

Zayd's hand in mine was steady, grounding, yet my heart raced like a bird desperate to escape its cage. I shouldn't have let him touch me. I shouldn't have even said his name. I was a wife, bound by vows spoken before the Gods and my family, tied to a man who gave me everything but joy. And yet... I never knew happiness until him.

Before Zayd, my voice had been little more than duty—a hymn sung for others, polished and hollow. With him, it was alive, trembling with color and truth. He made me remember I had a soul. He made me feel as though the songs in me were worth hearing.

I knew I was a fool for letting him come so close, for letting the world tilt toward him and away from everything else I was supposed to be. But I couldn't stop myself.

He rose slowly, guiding me with him, lifting me from the rocking chair. My feet barely touched the porch boards before his arm was around me, strong and sure, carrying me inside. The house felt different with him in it—warmer, more alive, as if the very walls leaned closer to hear the two of us breathe.

I lifted my hand, fingers brushing against the sharp line of his cheek, the roughness of his jaw. His skin was warm beneath my touch, and I felt the breath leave me in a shaky exhale. I brought him closer, pulling him down into a kiss I had no right to give, and yet it felt inevitable, written into the marrow of my bones.

His lips met mine with a hunger restrained, held back only by the tenderness in him, and I melted into it. My body leaned into his, always helpless to resist the way he drew me in.

The world narrowed to the press of his mouth, the taste of him, the heat of his breath. He guided me further, his hand at the small of my back as he laid me gently onto the bed, the old quilt cool against my skin. He loomed over me, and when our mouths met again, the kiss was deeper, hungrier, as though he had been starving for me just as I had for him.

And in that moment, the ache of guilt, the fear of being caught, all of it slipped away. There was only him—always *him*.

The dream cracked apart, scattering like glass underfoot, and I jolted awake to sunlight burning through the curtains, too bright for the headache clawing at the back of my skull. My throat was dry, the taste of last night's vodka clinging to it like ash.

"Zayd..." His name slipped out before I could stop it, thick with sleep, like some confession I hadn't meant to give. My eyes squeezed shut, trying to will the dream back, but all I got was the dull throb behind my temples reminding me of just how deep I'd drowned myself last night.

And then I noticed it. The weight. The warmth. My hand resting against someone's chest that wasn't mine.

Fuck.

The scent hit me first—something clean, something grounding, not the stale tang of liquor and regret I'd expected. My fingers curled, testing, and there it was: solid muscle, slow rise and fall. Real.

I cracked my eyes open, blinking hard at the light until the blur cleared. And there he was. *Him*.

"Zayd..." I whispered it again, but this time it burned, embarrassment flooding me as the fragments of the night slammed back into place. The shots. The bartender. My phone in my hand. And then—*fuck*—I'd called him. I actually fucking called him. For what? A hookup? To yell at him? I didn't even know.

And yet, here he was.

Zayd stirred beneath me, his hand lifting like it had always belonged there, palm cupping my cheek with an easy warmth that made my chest tighten. His eyes cracked open, blue and soft with sleep, and he smiled—slow, unhurried, devastating.

"Good morning." His voice was rough, deep with sleep, but threaded with something gentle. Something dangerous.

I groaned and buried my face against his chest, the cotton of his shirt cool against my skin, trying to hide from him, from myself, from all of it. "Gods..."

He laughed—quiet, low, brushing through me like a hand smoothing water. His fingers slid into my hair, slow and unthinking, and it was too much. Too natural. Like we'd done this a thousand times before.

"I'm sorry," I muttered against him, then turned my face so the words didn't drown in fabric. "I'm sorry for last night. You didn't have to stay. Honestly, you should've left, blocked my number, filed a restraining order." A rough laugh scraped out of me, sharp enough to make my head pound worse.

"You really weren't that bad," he said, voice soft but edged with that teasing note, the kind people use when they're trying to cushion the truth. "Besides... I had nothing better to do."

I tilted my head, eyes catching his. He was smiling, just barely, and something in me cracked. Before I could stop myself, the words were out. "If you have nothing better to do tomorrow... let me make it up to you."

I swallowed hard, forced myself not to flinch. "Let me take you out. A real date."

His hand stilled in my hair, and for a heartbeat the silence cut through me. Then his smile curved, faint but undeniable. "I can let you," he murmured, eyes half-lidded, that little grin pulling at his mouth. "But only if you promise me something."

"Anything," I said, too fast, already bracing for whatever condition he'd drop.

"You don't get drunk again." It was light, almost playful, but there was steel under it. A line drawn.

A huff of laughter broke out of me, half-genuine, half-exhausted. "I can promise that."

"Then it's a date," he said simply, and that smile—shit—that smile could've ruined me.

The water hit me like punishment. Scalding at first, then cooling as it ran off my skin, dripping in heavy rivulets down my chest, my back, pooling at my feet before slipping down the drain. I pressed my palms to the tile, shoulders hunched, letting the spray beat into me until my muscles ached. It wasn't cleansing. It was never cleansing. Just hot water, steam, and the same fucking weight clamped across my shoulders.

My father's funeral loomed like a noose. The families circling already, waiting to see which son would be crowned king of carrion. It shouldn't have been me anymore. Five years ago, maybe. But I'd walked away, and Legare didn't forgive walking away. The only reason I wasn't already a bullet in the ground was Alessia. My mother. She swore on her name I'd come back, swore I wasn't betraying anyone, that I just needed time. They wanted to believe her. They didn't believe me. And they were right not to.

I didn't want it then. Didn't want to be Cesare's shadow, another version of a man who thought blood was a language, who measured power by how much fear he could wring out of the room. That cycle—father, son, blood, dust—never ended. And I wanted out before it swallowed me whole.

But it had already started.

The water hit harder, stung against my back, and I saw him again. That kid. Eighteen, maybe. Still soft around the eyes, still carrying the kind of fear you don't know how to hide yet. He didn't belong there, not really. But that didn't matter. He was a liability, a spark in the wrong place, and in Legare sparks didn't get second chances.

Cesare's words cut through me even now: *"Douse the flame before it becomes a blaze."*

I had him. Close enough to finish it. And I let him go. Told him to run, not to look back. For a second I thought maybe that was it. Maybe I'd done something right. But Cesare always found them. Always. He dragged the boy back in front of me—half-dead, begging—and then he put the gun in my hand. Made me pull the trigger. Made me prove I wasn't weak.

The memory pressed harder than the water. His face. The sound. The silence after.

That's when the questions started. Not regret—no, that wasn't it. I wasn't sorry I did it. I was sorry I had to. And maybe that's worse. Maybe that's where the monster part comes in: not that I killed him, but that I convinced myself it was fine. That if the justification fit, the blood was clean.

I dragged my hands down my face, the water burning into my eyes, my mouth. Couldn't scrub it out. Couldn't scrub any of it out. The shower thundered around me like rain in a storm, but I could still hear it—the crack of the shot, the finality of it.

Was this really it? A life carved out in blood just to keep the wheel spinning, fear feeding fear? Was this supposed to be my peace?

I pressed my forehead to the tile, breath coming hard, the steam choking me like smoke. I didn't know if it scared me more that I hated it... or that some part of me thought it was the only thing I was ever good at.

The squeal of the shower handle cut through my silence, and the water died, leaving only the drip of it falling from my skin onto the tile. I stood there for a beat, chest heaving, heart still hammering like it hadn't realized the fight was over. Then I reached for the towel, dragging the cotton across my shoulders, down my arms, slow and deliberate. Like if I moved carefully enough, I could smooth the chaos back into order. But the storm didn't quiet. Not this time.

I had business to finish with Legare. Too many loose ends coiling at my feet, waiting to trip me. If I didn't cut them off now, they'd drag everything down with me. And Zayd couldn't see this. Not the part of me that still carried Cesare's world in my bones, that slipped back into violence like muscle memory. I didn't want to see his eyes turn cold, that softness gone, replaced by fear or worse—disgust.

This part of me had to stay buried.

I picked up my phone from the counter, the glass cool against my damp palm. My thumb hovered, brain stuttering, trying to piece together the fragments from last night. His name—his last name. It slid back into my mind eventually, heavy, inevitable.

Aristodemos.

I typed it in. Searched. Waited.

And there he was. Not a ghost, not a lie. Every detail he'd given me—true.

The punch landed low in my gut, sharp enough to make me wince. Guilt twisted hard, coiling tighter the longer I stared at his name glowing on my screen.

I am such an asshole.

Chapter Nine

Zayd

It had been centuries since I allowed myself to indulge in beauty crafted by mortal hands like this. Yet, even now, I could not resist the quiet call that beckoned me, drawing me in with a force both familiar and relentless. The Theion had shaped us, the Eudaimons, to be enamored by creation—by art, by music, by the small glimmers of divinity that mortals unknowingly threaded into their works. Perhaps it was meant as a reminder of the gods' own grandeur, a tether to their essence in this transient world. Our task was to guide, to bless, to walk unseen among mortals, bestowing their creations with the favor of heaven.

In the days long gone, we were a blessing, our wings a visible testament to the divine hand we served. Mortals would look upon us, some with reverence, others with fear, uncertain whether we came as harbingers of prosperity or warning—a need for protection for what's to come. But it was never ours to decide.

Even when the divide between the realms were not as wide, we were meant to stay apart. Our charge was simply to remain detached, untouched by the fleeting joys and sorrows that painted the human soul.

Philetos had been my charge.

I should have remained untouched, yet how could I? How could anyone with breath and sense not fall for the way music spilled from him like water from a sacred spring, or the way his laughter swirled through the air like a song born of stars? His compositions had stirred something ancient within me, something I had been fashioned to admire, but forbidden to hold. Perhaps it was always meant to be my undoing—crafted to love beauty, yet punished when that love strayed from reverence to desire.

I failed the gods. And in doing so, I failed him.

For my disobedience, we faded into the background of history, our once open presence reduced to myth and stories whispered to children at night. We became the silent overseers, watching from the fringes of Khaos, our influence still woven into the world but never again felt directly. The Kakodaimon, though—they were not bound by such limitations. They continued to walk among humans, reveling in their misfortune, growing stronger with each act of corruption or violence. No longer the grotesque creatures of old, they blended effortlessly into the modern world, using its inventions—its greed, its ambition—to twist mortals toward their own downfall.

"Am I boring you?" Silas' voice cut through my reverie, drawing me back from the edges of my own mind. I hadn't realized I'd been staring at the same painting for so long.

His words were soft, but there was an undercurrent there, something unsure. When I glanced at him, I noticed the way his fingers idly traced the stem of his wine glass, brows furrowed slightly as though he were worried he'd lost my attention.

"No," I murmured, almost too softly. "Not bored."

Bored? How could I be bored with you by my side?

I glanced around us, at the gallery he'd rented out for the night, just for the two of us to enjoy alone. Its walls were filled with art awaiting its upcoming exhibition. It was hard to fathom anyone being anything less than enchanted by the effort he had gone to.

I let my gaze return to the painting before us—a celestial figure, its wings wide and filled with light, its face a mask of serene, unreadable emotion. It reminded me of the old days, of a time when we were seen not as relics but as beings who still walked among the living. The gold leaf that lined the figure's wings caught the light just right, making it seem as though the entire painting shimmered, as though it were alive. I couldn't help but think of my kin, of what we had lost, and of what I had once been.

I stepped closer, drawn in by the details. I could feel Silas beside me, his presence solid and warm. He didn't say anything, but his nearness grounded me in a way I hadn't expected.

"The brushstrokes," I murmured, tracing the air before the painting with my fingers, as if I could feel the texture of the paint itself. "The colors... they're like nothing I've seen in a long time." I tilted my head, letting the emotion simmer just beneath my words.

"It's truly something," he said, his voice more casual, but I could hear the thoughtfulness in it, the way he respected the beauty before him, even if he didn't see it the same way I did.

As we stood there, I found myself stealing glances at him, watching the way the evening light softened his features, how his usually sharp, confident demeanor had a gentleness to it now, something quieter.

His gaze found mine as though he felt the weight of my eyes upon him, as though he knew that I had been watching him. Silas stepped closer, his chest brushing softly against my shoulder, the warmth of him spilling over me like sunlight after a long, cold night. And then, his hand—steady, sure—cupped the side of my face, the roughness of his palm a contrast to the tenderness in his touch.

There was no hesitation in him. Only certainty. Only the quiet, unwavering kind of affection that had the power to level empires, that had already laid me low so many times before. His lips found mine with the ease of something long-remembered, as though they had always been destined to meet. I let my eyes fall shut, giving myself to the moment, to the softness of him, to the heady blend of wine on our breaths, the scent of leather and spice clinging to his clothes.

Memories washed over me like the tide—every kiss, every touch, every glance we had shared across time. In every life, in every reincarnation, I had loved him. And this version of him—Silas—was no different. He had taken root in me just as deeply, just as completely, as Philetos had the first time.

If only I had known that this time would be different. If I had known that seeing him again would sever the bond differently from all the other times. I would have come sooner. I would have torn the veil between us, if it meant I could have held him in my arms just one moment earlier. Regret coiled in my chest, bitter and sharp. How many years this time around had been wasted, lost to hesitation and fear that his death would come shortly after meeting?

I tilted my head, leaning into him, deepening the kiss. The sides of our noses brushed as we pressed closer, my heart a wild drumbeat in my chest. I could feel the rhythm of his pulse, steady and sure, beating in time with mine. This was my heaven, my Aither. My love. It had always been him. In every life, our souls had been woven together.

He pulled back just slightly, his forehead resting against mine, the world narrowing to the soft brush of his breath against my skin. When I opened my eyes, I found his closed, his expression serene yet vulnerable. His voice, when he spoke, was a whisper of velvet, something fragile and intimate. "There's just something about you. I... do you believe in soulmates?" Silas chuckled softly, cheeks flushed. "That was... cheesy."

"It's not," I said softly, the words caught between a smile and something far more painful. My nose grazed his gently. "I do believe in soulmates." I want him to say it, the plea rising in me unbidden. Say you feel it, too. Say you remember our love. But the fear slithered through me, cold and gnawing—what if the bond truly had only broken prematurely, and once he realized, once he named the truth aloud, the Theion would take him from me again? That was how it always went. They gave him to me, only to rip him away once the realization came.

But this time, I would know how it would end. The Callaghans. They would be the ones to end him, to tear him from me once more.

I couldn't let it happen. Not again. Without the bond, I couldn't track him like I once had. I couldn't feel his presence in the same way, couldn't follow the thread of his breath, his life. I had to stay close, had to remain at his side, whether in Khaos or in the mortal realm. I was already damned. The Theion had forsaken me long ago. I would not let another version of him be taken. I will take that premature snap as a blessing, it had given me time to prepare and perhaps even prevent.

Silas kissed me again, this time with more urgency, more fervor. His body pressed against mine, pushing me back half a step, his arm wrapping around my waist to pull me closer, as if afraid I might slip away. The movement caused his wine to spill from the glass, but neither of us cared. I pulled back only to bury my face against his neck, breathing in the scent of him, my lips brushing the pulse that beat there. His hand slid from my cheek to the back of my head, fingers tangling gently in my hair.

"Silas," I whispered, voice thick with reluctance, "I don't think this is the place for this."

"Does that mean I have permission to take you somewhere else?" His fingers tightened slightly in my hair, just enough to draw my face up from the hollow of his neck, forcing my gaze to meet his. His eyes were dark, intent, filled with something unspoken yet heavy between us.

The air around us thickened, a slow, coiling tension wrapping us in its embrace. My chest rose and fell as I searched his face, my heart pounding in time with the desire that thrummed through my veins. I wanted to be undone by him, ruined by the mortal who had always undone me. He was the reason I had fallen, the reason I had lost my place among the divine. He had always been my undoing, and I welcomed it everytime.

"Yes," I breathed.

And in that single word, I surrendered.

Chapter Ten

Silas

Why did it already feel so damn easy with him? From the first word out of his mouth, it was like something had locked into place, like a puzzle piece I didn't even know I was missing until he showed up and filled it. Fate, maybe. Though I'd never put much stock in fate. Still—there was something in the way it all fit too neatly, too quick, like the universe had set it up just to watch me stumble.

And underneath that ease, the pull—it gnawed at me. The reminder of the life I kept tucked away, the one I hadn't shown him. The blood, the weight of a name that carried more shadows than pride. If I dragged that world into the open, would he stay? Or would he look at me the way they all eventually did—like I was something to fear? Worse—what if naming it out loud dragged it closer, like speaking a curse into being?

The night air cooled the heat running through me as we stepped out of the gallery. The evening was calm, the town's streets empty save for the faint scent of salt and seaweed that clung to the breeze. It felt good to be back here, away from the chaos of LA and all the twisted memories that came with it. It was cleaner here, easier to breathe. I could almost lie to myself and believe this town would let me disappear. That I could keep Zayd untouched by the rest of it.

Then we rounded the corner, and the lie broke apart.

Someone was sitting on the hood of my car. Not sitting—waiting. Sleeves rolled up, tattoos black and winding across his forearms, a gun dangling from his hand like it was just another accessory. The dying sun hit the steel, making it flare, real and cold in the quiet.

His eyes caught mine as he slid off the car, every step deliberate, like a man who wanted me to see him coming. The lot was empty. Just him, me, and Zayd.

"Stay behind me," I said, my voice low, steady, like my pulse wasn't already kicking against my ribs. "And don't say a word."

I moved quicker, cutting the distance before he could close it on us. My smile was easy, practiced, the kind that smoothed out the edges of a threat, made me look unbothered. Inside, my instincts were coiled tight, waiting for the strike.

"A bit forward, don't you think?" I drawled, letting my gaze drag down his arm to the gun before slipping back to his face. "Planting your ass on another man's hood without asking first." I didn't bother hiding the double edge in my voice.

Up close, I could see it—he wasn't one of my father's men. Didn't carry that weight in his shoulders. Not Callaghan, not one of the other families I knew either. But five years was a long time to be gone. Long enough for new wolves to take old ground.

His eyes—green, sharp, mean—cut to Zayd. Instinct had me shift, blocking his line of sight before he could get a good look. The sneer spread slow across his face, his words thick with that Irish accent. "So this is why you ran, little Legare prince. Because Cesare's son can't carry on the line with his frociaggine. Poor fuckin' sap."

My tongue pressed to my cheek, and I smirked, dry laughter catching in my throat. He butchered the word so badly it almost offended me more than the insult itself. That lilt nailed it—Callaghan. *Of course.*

I didn't waste time trading words. My fist connected with his jaw, bone cracking under the blow. His head snapped back, his balance teetered, but only for a breath before the gun came up. I lunged, tackling him, dragging us both to the ground in a mess of limbs and concrete burn. My knee crushed his wrist, pinning the gun down, while his free hand found my ribs. Pain thudded through me, sharp, but the adrenaline washed it out before it could stick.

My knuckles slammed into his nose. The crunch was satisfying—ugly, wet, final. Blood sprayed across my hand, spattering onto my lips, copper hot and bitter on my tongue. Rage surged like a tide, and I leaned in, my fingers wrapping his throat, feeling the frantic beat of his pulse under my grip.

"It's pronounced *frociaggine*," I hissed, tightening until his breath stuttered, until his eyes bulged just slightly. "Fucking dumbass." I released just enough to drive another fist into his face. His blood slickened my hand, and I squeezed again, harder, the world narrowing to the sound of his choking breaths and the rush in my ears.

He swung up at me, fists desperate, but I barely felt it. None of it mattered. Not him, not the Callaghans, not the old wars dragging themselves back out of the dirt. I just wanted quiet. A life where I didn't have to bleed or make others bleed just to breathe.

And then Zayd flashed through my head—clear, startling, cutting through the red haze. His eyes. His voice. The fragile, impossible thing we were starting to build.

My grip faltered. Just a fraction.

It was enough.

He ripped an arm free, the gun swinging up, steel cracking into the side of my skull. Pain burst white-hot, my vision shattering, tilting. The world collapsed inward, edges going black, sound hollowing out.

Figures my peace would cost me this.

And then—nothing.

I woke to the drag of linen against my skin, the faint musk of old wood crowding the air. My skull throbbed with every heartbeat, each pulse like a hammer blow reverberating through bone. My tongue tasted of iron, bitter and stale, the memory of blood refusing to fade. When I raised a hand to my temple, pain lanced sharp and immediate, flaring down into my ribs. Breathing hurt. Moving hurt. Existing hurt.

"Stay still."

Zayd's voice cut through the fog—quiet, precise, impossible to ignore. He sat at the edge of the bed, his presence steady, though his eyes avoided mine. "I haven't cleaned your head yet," he said, flat but not unfeeling. His gaze skimmed over the bruises, the split skin, cataloguing every damage like he could will it away by knowing it. His mouth was tight, carved into a line that betrayed more than his words ever would. "You've likely got a concussion. Your ribs—bruised, maybe cracked."

I studied him. The set of his shoulders, the way his eyes moved without landing, as though I might shatter if he looked too closely. My mistakes had caught up to me, dragged him into the undertow, and for once, the consequence wasn't mine alone to bear.

My hand moved before thought. I caught his wrist, my fingers tightening, desperate for proof—his pulse thrumming beneath skin, steady and alive. "Were you hurt?" My voice scraped raw, gravel in my throat.

He shook his head, hair falling forward until he pushed it back with a careless flick. "Let me clean you up, alright?" His eyes finally met mine, and it felt like being held under water. There was weight there—concern, yes, but something else beneath it. Judgment? Doubt? The beginning of an ending I wasn't ready to face.

My chest tightened, and rage stirred in me, useless and misdirected. I wanted to curse Cesare. Even in death he was here, pulling the strings, sending his wolves to remind me I could never truly leave.

Zayd slipped free, his wrist sliding from my grip like water. He rose and crossed the room, the sound of running water spilling from the bathroom sink. I watched the small tremor in his hands as he wrung out the cloth, the tension in his shoulders like a storm about to break.

I pushed myself up, pain gnawing through bone and muscle, every step an accusation written into my flesh. But I couldn't stay prone, couldn't let the distance widen between us. Not like this. Not when the thought of him walking away already felt like a blade pressed to my throat.

I stepped in behind him, so close I could feel the heat bleeding off his body, the taut line of his back stiff with unspoken tension. Instinct overruled thought—I slid an arm around his waist, drawing him flush to me, my chest pressed hard against his spine. His breath caught, sharp and quick, and our eyes met in the mirror. His blue, steady; mine, searching.

"Do I disgust you now?" My voice came out low, hushed, like I didn't want the room itself to hear the answer.

"Silas." He exhaled my name, soft but heavy, his gaze dropping back to the sink. "Go lie down."

But I couldn't. Not yet. Maybe not ever.

"Zayd." His name slipped out quieter this time, a plea dressed as a whisper. My hand rose, cupping his jaw, tilting his face back toward the mirror, back toward me. "Do you fear me now?"

His eyes held mine, unwavering, oceans pulling me deeper. I braced myself for it—for disgust, for fear, for the fracture I knew I deserved. But there was nothing of the sort. Just that maddening calm, that steadiness that belonged only to him.

"No," he said finally, quiet, certain. "Such feelings could never stir within me for you. I'm not going anywhere, Silas."

The knot in my chest loosened so suddenly it hurt. Relief—or possession—I couldn't tell the difference. "Good," I rasped, the word rough in my throat. And truth be told, I wasn't sure I would've let him walk away even if he'd wanted to. He lived in me now, haunted my days, claimed my nights. The thought of losing him felt like suffocation.

I leaned to him, lips brushing the slope of his neck, tasting salt, heat, skin. My hand lingered on his chest, fingers splayed as though I could keep him anchored there. Beautiful, I thought—ruinously, dangerously beautiful. A masterpiece I had no right to touch.

My other hand drifted down, unhurried, to the buttons of his shirt. One by one, slow, deliberate, I worked them loose, my gaze never leaving the mirror. His lips parted, his breath shallow, trembling, and I watched every flicker of it like a man starved.

His hand rose, weakly gripping my forearm, the touch more plea than resistance. He wanted to stop me—or maybe he only wanted to pretend he did. His body betrayed him, trembling under my touch, yielding even as he tried to hold on.

"Let me have more of you," I whispered against his ear, the words a vow, a demand, both. My hand slid from his jaw to his throat, fingers tightening just enough to feel the frantic beat of his pulse. His grip faltered. He melted. And I unfastened the belt at his waist, slipping beneath the fabric to claim him.

Hard already, straining against my palm, his quiet groan tore through the air between us, low and guttural, and it split something inside me wide open. My thumb dragged across his slit, slow and deliberate, spreading the wetness there, and I forced him to look—eyes locked with mine in the mirror. "Look at you," I murmured, voice dark, reverent. "So wet for me already."

His head fell back against my shoulder, throat bared, lips parted. His eyes fluttered half-shut as I stroked him, at first a tease—leisurely, cruelly slow—before settling into a rhythm that wrung shudders out of him. Every gasp, every hitch of his breath fed something feral in me. The heat between us thickened.

I pressed my mouth to his neck, tracing the line of his pulse with my lips before sinking my teeth into his skin, marking him. He said he wasn't going anywhere, but I needed him to carry me with him regardless, etched into his body, his blood, his breath. If he left, I wanted him branded. I wanted him ruined.

His fingers tangled in my hair, tugging, desperate, as his body went taut beneath my touch. I felt him unravel in my grip, the twitch of his cock, the sharp intake of breath, the inevitability of it.

He broke with a soft, shattered moan, spilling cum across my hand, streaking the mirror in white. I held him through it, never looking away, watching in the reflection as his face contorted, flushed and undone, his chest heaving, his body trembling.

Beautiful.

No. Not beautiful. Beauty was too tame, too shallow a word. This wasn't beauty—it was ruin. It was the raw truth of him, unfiltered and unguarded, a man surrendering to lust with nothing left to hide. That was what I craved. That was what hollowed me out and filled me all at once.

Some men worship gods. They pray for salvation, for meaning, for purpose. But *this*—this is what I want to worship. Zayd was my religion, his pleasure my holy purpose. I would give anything, everything, to keep him, to make him mine forever.

The roar of the crowd had been its own symphony, surging like a tide against the hall's velvet walls. My hands still quivered with the echo of the piano keys, with the thunder that had risen to meet me. I should have basked in it. I should have let the music linger. But then—

A scream.

It cut through the air, sharp and raw, louder than any note I had played. Smoke billowed across the rafters, black and thick, swallowing the chandeliers whole. The hall erupted. Men in tailored coats and women in silk gowns fought toward the doors, their polished shoes slipping on marble, their cries rising into a discordant hymn. The fire spread, red and hungry, licking its way across the curtains, devouring everything.

Heat seared my skin. My chest burned, each breath dragging smoke like knives into my lungs. I staggered, tried for the doors, but the ceiling groaned and split above me. A beam came crashing down, splitting the path in two, sparks spitting across the floor. The way out was gone.

Panic tore through me, bitter and choking. I stumbled against the piano I had just played, the lacquered surface already blistering in the heat. "Help!" My voice broke on ash. "Zayd!"

I didn't know why I called for him. Didn't know how his name had rooted itself in my throat, but the moment it left me, he was there. Out of the smoke, out of the fire, untouched by flame, untaken by ruin. His coat trailed behind him as though the inferno bent to let him pass. But his eyes—his eyes were a storm undone.

"Alaric—" His voice cracked as he reached me. His hands caught me as my knees gave way, pulling me hard against his chest. My head fell to his shoulder, every breath shattering, ragged, the smoke tearing through me like glass.

"I—don't—" The words broke, too thin to form.

"Don't speak," he begged, voice breaking as he pressed his face into my neck, as if hiding me from the fire could save me. His tears seared hotter than the flames. "Not again. Please, not you."

My thoughts splintered, scattered, everything dimming at the edges. I blinked, and his face swam in and out of focus. "Why—why are you crying?" My lips barely moved, confusion clinging heavier than the smoke. "Zayd..."

"I'm sorry," he whispered, again and again, a litany pressed into my skin, as though the words themselves could bind me to this world. His arms shook around me, as if he could hold me back from the inevitable.

The fire howled. The rafters split and fell. And still, he clung to me like a man already mourning.

I woke with a violent jolt, lungs clawing for air. I moved to sit, hunched on the edge of the bed, breath ragged, ribs screaming with each rise of my chest. My palms pressed hard into my thighs as if grounding myself could drag me out of whatever the hell that had been. A dream. That's all it was supposed to be. Just a dream.

But it didn't feel like one.

The phantom sting of smoke still clawed at my lungs, each cough echoing in my ribs, sharp enough to make my vision blur. My skin was damp, clammy, as though I'd been standing in the fire myself, heat blistering against me. And beneath it all, worse than the ache, worse than the panic, was the heaviness of it.

I dragged my hands up over my face, gripping hard at my temples. *What the fuck was wrong with me?* Why did it still feel real?

It was madness. Had to be. I'd never been one to indulge in fantasies or omens, never cared for that spiritual bullshit my mother's side of the family liked to whisper about in hushed tones. But the way the world had bled into me just now—the smell, the heat, the weight of someone else's death pressing against my ribs—how was I supposed to explain that away?

I leaned forward, elbows braced on my knees, the room spinning faintly in the dark. My pulse thundered, uneven, restless. What was happening to me? Was I losing it?

I shut my eyes tight, but the images wouldn't leave me. Smoke. Fire. Splintering beams.

For the first time in years, maybe longer, I wondered if I was going mad.

Chapter Eleven

Zayd

Eryx's voice, though carrying the usual teasing edge, was softer today, his words lacking the customary mischief. He traced idle patterns along the temple's ancient stone, his eyes fixed on something distant, something I couldn't reach. "Your human seems to be falling for you fast this time," he said, the corner of his mouth twitching, but the usual spark was absent.

He had been unusually quiet, his boldness subdued, his mind elsewhere. He wasn't wrong, though. Silas was falling fast. It was inevitable. But it wasn't something I could indulge in fully—not when the weight of eternity pressed down upon me. "You know the will is going to name him, right?" Eryx continued, finally meeting my gaze, as if he'd been waiting for me to say something, to respond to the thoughts that lingered between us. "It doesn't matter if he was absent. He's the eldest. That's just how they've always done it. Tradition."

"I know," I replied, the words leaving my lips with the heaviness of a sigh. Silas had been trying to keep me away from his family's affairs, unaware that I already knew more than he could imagine. He had been so relieved when I hadn't fled after the incident in the gallery parking lot, as if my staying was the only thing that mattered. But he hadn't asked why I stayed. Why I wasn't repelled. He was slipping. A man like him, with his past, should have been more wary of someone like me. But no—he was blinded by his own relief, his own desire to believe that I could be the one thing in his life untainted by blood and violence.

Even when I told him that the police had been called by a bystander, he didn't question it. Didn't question me. It was dangerous, this sloppiness. And I could only hope his family would take notice and pass the mantle of Legare to Augustus, sparing Silas from the weight of that world.

I looked toward the entrance of the temple, my patience worn thin by the passage of time. "Are you sure this is the time Malaika said to meet her?" The words tasted bitter in my mouth. Every moment we lingered felt like a gamble. If I wanted to keep Silas alive, keep us together in this lifetime, I needed to be near him.

"There she is," Eryx murmured with a grin as Malaika appeared, her figure materializing in the temple's heart as if summoned by my words. She moved with the ancient grace of a celestial. Even in her silence, there was a regal air about her, as though she carried the weight of the cosmos within her gaze.

I stepped forward, the distance between us closing, though I remained cautious, the urgency in my movements betraying the calm I tried to maintain. "Did you speak to the other Daimons?"

Her voice was like the brush of wind through leaves, poised and elegant. "I said I would, and I did. There's an imbalance. Philetos' soul is the cause." She said, her words blunt and straight to the point.

My pulse quickened. "But it is the Theion who created this imbalance," I replied sharply, unable to keep the edge from my voice. The gods. It always came back to them.

Malaika's eyes flickered with something unreadable, her tone unwavering. "No, Zayd. You are the one who created this imbalance. Not the gods. We are given tools, knowledge, and freedom. But with freedom comes responsibility. The Theion judge when we stray. And you strayed, Zayd. Let's not forget that."

Her words struck with the precision of a blade, each syllable a reminder of my fall. Once, I would have abandoned everything for the will of the Theion. Their ways had been my ways, their thoughts my own. But now, standing before Malaika, I couldn't shake the sense that it was they who were wrong. Or had my judgment fallen so far that I couldn't see reason?

"Alright, enough of this," Eryx interjected, his usual levity absent, his tone cutting through the tension. "We'll just keep going in circles if we continue like this. Speak plainly, Malaika. What is wrong with the soul bond?"

"The soul tie is gone because the soul is wearing thin," she said, her words measured, the truth she carried in them heavier than anything else in this cursed temple. "Philetos has reached the end of his cycle."

The end of his cycle. A mortal soul could only be renewed so many times before it was lost to the mists of Erebos forever. Philetos had lived more lives than most, but each one had been cut short, torn away before its time.

Some mortal souls are measured by a different scale, deemed precious enough to be granted the rare grace of eternity, transformed into Daimons. I've never understood or even remembered why Eryx and I were chosen for this. Whatever virtue or vice we embodied in our mortal lives, I cannot imagine it to be more significant than what Philetos gave the world. If there is any justice, any wisdom in the gods' design, he would have been the one to receive such a gift—a life unending, a place among us.

Malaika's gaze held mine. "The mists will come for your Silas soon."

The world seemed to tilt, the temple walls closing in around me. "I refuse to accept that," I said, my voice quieter than I intended, the weight of my words falling against the stone floor. "Take me to Aither. I need to speak to the Theion."

I needed to beg. There was no other way. Philetos had been my reason for enduring, my tether to this existence. The thought of a world without him, without the hope of his inevitable return, was unbearable.

"As I've told you before, Zayd, a Daimon cannot simply request an audience with the Theion," Malaika said, her lips pressing into a thin line, though there was a softness in her voice, a warning. "However, there are Theion within your reach." I could sense her sympathy towards me, and this was her way of giving me something. Some hope.

"You can't mean..." Eryx began, but his grin betrayed his thoughts. "Well, little Eudai, how badly do you want that audience?"

I stared at him, the weight of his words pressing down on me. I felt lost, as if the very ground beneath me had shifted. What were they talking about?

"The Theion in Erebos are not unreachable," Eryx continued, his chuckle cutting through the tension like a blade. "They roam the mists with the dead and the Kakodaimons. I don't know why I didn't think of it before."

"Because Eudaimon aren't meant to be in Erebos," I said, my arms crossing over my chest. "Just as Kakodaimon aren't meant to be in Aither."

Eryx's grin widened. "Then I guess that means we'll just have to be sneaky, won't we?"

I would have known Eryx in any form he chose to take. Whether cloaked in mortal skin or bathed in shadows, the essence of him never wavered. The way his eyes glinted—silvered like the edge of a blade catching moonlight—was unmistakably his, even in the form he wore now. They say the eyes are windows to the soul, and for Daimons, there is no greater truth. In this form, Eryx's gaze held the same gleam, that playful defiance, though now wrapped in something far more formidable.

He was massive, his body a hulking silhouette of muscle and sinew, dark gray and unyielding as stone. Horns, black as night, spiraled from his head. His hands—clawed, powerful—gripped me easily as he pulled me into his side, a silent gesture of protection. A vast, bat-like wing furled around me, darkening my view of the path ahead, leaving me with nothing but the steady rhythm of his breath and the pressure of his presence to guide me through the depths of Erebos.

This place was nothing like the realm above, where the air sang with light and life. Here, there was only the endless, oppressive murmur of forgotten souls, a constant whisper that seemed to seep into the bones. Erebos, the realm of shadows and echoes, where the dead relived their most potent memories—some bound to eternal bliss, others condemned to endless torment. It was a reflection, a twisted mirror of Aither's radiance. Where Aither bathed in light, Erebos drowned in darkness. And yet, they were two halves of a whole, inseparable by design, the Theion's eternal need for balance written into the very fabric of these realms.

The mists of Erebos clung to everything here, swirling in the dimness of the lower realm, carrying with them the weight of a thousand lifetimes. I could hear the murmur of souls, distant and close, stories playing over and over—some filled with joy, others marked by pain. It was unsettling in its constancy, an endless cycle of remembrance, and punishment.

My gaze shifted upward, finding Eryx. Even in this form, there was a strange beauty to him—a feral, primal grace in the sharp lines of his body, in the way his wings curled protectively around me. My hand twitched, reaching upward almost on instinct, fingertips hovering near his jaw, just shy of touching. But before I could act on the impulse, he spoke, his voice low and direct, cutting through the air between us. "We're close now," he said, his eyes trained on the path ahead. "There's a pool—silent, unlike the rest of this place. The Theion favor it, probably because it's a link to Aither. There will be one waiting."

I nodded, the word "Catoptron" slipping from my lips in a breath. A pool that bridges Erebos and Aither. The waters of Catoptron only bend to the will of the Theion. I had seen its counterpart in Aither once, shimmering with light that seemed to ripple across eternity. It sang a song that was the embodiment of expression. But here, the silence of that pool must be a mercy, a brief reprieve from the cacophony of souls.

We hadn't taken more than a few steps when a voice called out, resonant and strange, shifting from masculine to feminine with an eerie fluidity. "Eryx... and Zayd, how unexpected." The voice was unmistakable, a sound that stirred ancient memories. Theion.

Eryx's grip loosened, his wing unfurling to reveal me fully to the depths of the realm. Around us, the eyes of

Kakodaimons gleamed, their presence a dark, lingering force just beyond the edges of my sight. But it was the figure in the pool that drew my attention, the Theion—its form indistinct, an outline more than a body, neither male nor female, yet containing the essence of both. The water it bathed in was darker than the void, deeper than the realm itself.

"Theion," Eryx murmured, bending to one knee, his head bowing low. I followed suit, lowering myself with a reverence that felt more like submission than respect.

The voice shifted again, cool and detached, yet somehow intimate. "It is unheard of to see an Eudaimon here. What brings you to this place?"

My gaze flicked to the pool, to the still, dark surface. "Do I truly need to speak? You know why I've come." My voice was steady, but weariness clung to the edges. I was exhausted, and the weight of this place, my reason for being here, pressed down on me.

The Theion's eyes—if they could be called that—settled on me. "Philetos." The name rippled through the water like a stone cast into a still pond. The Theion stood, its form shifting as it stepped toward the edge, closer. "You seek to keep your lover's soul from the mists."

"Yes." The word was barely a whisper, swallowed by the darkness around us.

"Do you know the purpose of the Daimon, Zayd?" The question was rhetorical, a prelude to the lesson I had heard before. "They are the balance. Eudaimon and Kakodaimon—two sides of the same coin, the hands of the divine. One to push, one to pull. One to destroy, one to restore. It is through them that order is maintained."

"I understand," I said, though the words felt hollow. "But what does that have to do with Philetos?"

The Theion's steps were slow, deliberate, the pool's edge now just beneath its feet. "The balance was broken when you fell, Zayd. When you bound yourself to him, to Philetos. You upset the scales, forcing his soul into a cycle it was never meant to endure. And now, it must be corrected."

The Theion reached out, its hand brushing my cheek with a touch that was far too gentle for the gravity of its words. "His soul must join the mists. It has been given too many chances."

I swallowed, my jaw tight. "Can't you let him live this one mortal life? All the others have been cut short—"

"Because of you," the Theion interrupted, its tone never wavering, soft and calm as if stating an undeniable fact. "You interfered. You couldn't let him be, and so the cycle repeated, life taken before its time, over and over again."

I clenched my teeth, the guilt I had always carried now a searing weight in my chest. I had known. I had always known. But hearing it spoken aloud, from the lips of the Theion—it was a truth too heavy to bear. I had doomed him, again and again.

"The mists of Erebos will claim Silas soon." The Theion's words echoed Malaika's haunting warning. "It cannot be undone. Fate will have its due. Enjoy what little time remains, Zayd. In time, you will forget him. This is but a blink in your eternal life. When you have accepted that, you will be welcomed home."

I closed my eyes, leaning into the Theion's touch despite myself, despite the bitterness of the truth. There was no denying what I was—what I had done. Philetos would be lost to me again, and I... I would be left to endure.

Chapter Twelve

Silas

Five years. That's how long it had been since I set foot in this room—my childhood room. It felt smaller now, shrunken, like a stage abandoned by its actors, the curtains still half-drawn, the lines still hanging in the air. And I was the only one left to recite them, a man of thirty dressing in the same four walls where I once thought the future stretched wide enough to escape.

The suit hung stiff across my shoulders, foreign against my skin. Dressing for my father's funeral—never something I imagined, not because I thought him immortal, but because I trained myself not to think of him at all. His death wasn't supposed to matter. Caring was dangerous, and I had spent my life learning how to sever it clean.

I never wanted this. Not the legacy. Not the title. Not the weight of his name pressed into my spine like chains. And yet inevitability crept in all the same. I was his heir. His cunning. His hunger. His violence. As natural to me as breathing. And still, I left. I carved out my exile, shed his skin like it could rot in the ground without me.

The floorboard outside groaned—a sound I'd once learned to fear in this house where footsteps never meant peace. Two knocks followed, soft, almost uncertain. I slid the jacket on, buttoned it, and crossed to the oak door.

"Madre wanted me to see if you were ready," August's voice came, flat through the wood. When I opened the door, he wouldn't meet my eyes. "The service is in an hour. She wants us to ride together."

"August." I said his name low, forcing him to lift his gaze, to see what had been festering between us all these years. Wrong time, maybe. But when would it ever be the right one? "I'm sorry. I wasn't abandoning you. I just... needed out."

His stare was hard, cutting through apology like it meant nothing. "I can forgive you for leaving," he said, voice even but sharp with hurt. "But not for never coming back."

So it was the time, whether I wanted it or not.

"What was I supposed to do? Sweep you out of here like some savior? I was grown, August. And so were you. You could've left, too."

His eyes lit with anger, the kind that had been steeping for years. "You think I had the choice? That I could just walk away? I'm not *you*, Silas. He wouldn't have let me. And I wasn't leaving her behind. Not like *you did*."

The words struck where they always would. I flinched but didn't move. "August—"

"Don't." His hand lifted, keeping me at a distance as if space could dull the edge of what he carried. "You're back now, and it doesn't matter. You'll wear Legare's shadow until you die, same as he did. His legacy is yours. That's how it always was."

I caught his arm before he could pull away. "I don't want it. Any of it."

His laugh was humorless, a breath of resignation. He tore free, eyes finally meeting mine with something colder than anger. "You don't get to want. You're a Vassallo. Start acting like one."

And then he was gone, leaving me in the doorway, choking on a name that would never loosen its grip.

"Let's go," he called back, not turning, not waiting.

And I followed—because maybe he was right. Maybe choice was never part of the bloodline.

The silence hit me as soon as I stepped inside—not reverent, not holy, just heavy. Thick enough to choke on, thick with their stares. The kind of silence that doesn't let you forget you're being watched. *Cesare's eldest returns. Undeserving.* And, from a few of the younger faces I didn't recognize, probably a simple: *Who the fuck is that?*

I almost laughed. What a reunion.

The faces blurred—half familiar, half strangers wearing familiar expressions. But the bones of the room were the same: four families gathered like wolves circling carrion, Legare knitted into the marrow of it all. And me—the ghost of an heir, dragged back to play a part I never auditioned for. My name still carried weight, though whether it would hold or break, I could see it gleaming in their eyes.

Would I take it on? Could I? Should I?

Questions I'd been asking myself long before this moment, and still had no answer for.

I'd wanted something else once. Something quieter, smaller, softer. For a heartbeat, I could almost smell the cheap beer, hear the low murmur of my bar, the thrum of his laugh under it all—Zayd.

Gods, not here. Not now. Not when I needed to look like grief instead of longing.

We moved as one, August and I bracketing our mother, her arms looped through ours like delicate chains. The urn sat waiting on its pedestal, black marble dressed in flowers and rosaries, as if ornaments could make his death respectable.

A heart attack. That's what they said. Cesare Vassallo—my father, the man who could gut someone with his eyes—taken down not by a rival or a bullet, but by cholesterol. It felt like the universe was making a joke, and for once, I wasn't laughing.

I stared at the urn, gaudy and gleaming. Would Zayd call it beautiful? Or see it the way I did—an overpriced paperweight dressed up like legacy. The corner of my mouth twitched, the humor sharp and fleeting, gone before anyone could see.

The ceremony dragged, one hollow condolence after another. Voices blurred into smoke, shapeless and cloying, a language of obligation more than grief. They weren't mourning Cesare the man—they were mourning Cesare the shadow, the power vacuum his death had left behind.

And me? I hadn't come for him. I came because I had to. Because I was the oldest. Because tradition demanded I stand here, waiting for a crown I never wanted to fall on my head like a guillotine blade.

The flowers, the rosaries, the careful theater of it all—none of it mattered. Cesare hadn't belonged to God in years. Power had claimed him long before death did.

As the crowd thinned, the hum of mourning dulled into something sharper. Grief was an opening act; the real performance came after. The whispers shifted, the air itself tilting as the true gathering began—the heads of the families, the ones who fed on empire, not sentiment, slipping into a smaller room like vultures to bone.

I followed, my mother's hand light on my arm, her touch both tender and tethering. August stalked on my other side, posture stiff as though he could iron his way through it. We looked like soldiers marching into a war already lost.

The room was heavy with eyes. Arnaldo stood at the far end, arms folded, a sentinel carved in stone. The other heads sat in silence, their gazes sharp, cutting, measuring. I could feel the weight of it—all of them waiting for me to play heir.

My mother took her chair, graceful, deliberate. I followed, August to my right. Then the lawyer spoke, voice flat:

"Vassallo assets remain Vassallo assets," he said, as though the empire we were discussing was a mere line item in a ledger. "The fortune, the real estate, the properties..." It all felt so clinical. Like we weren't discussing who would take over this criminal empire, like it was just a simple business. I almost laughed at the absurdity of it.

"When it comes to Mr. Vassallo's company, it is well known the ownership must remain with a blood relative, as it has for generations," the lawyer continued, his voice a monotone hum.

My gaze flicked to August. Could I give it to him? Should I? Would he even want it? The thought gnawed at me as the lawyer's voice droned on.

The words I had been waiting for—dreading, maybe—finally came.

"Cesare's will states that ownership is to be passed to Silas Vassallo. His eldest son."

I knew it. Of course I knew it. But knowing and hearing aren't the same. The weight of it still struck like a blow, an invisible hand tightening around my throat.

And before I could stop myself, the words slipped out:

"What if I refuse?"

The air snapped. The lawyer froze. My mother's eyes—sharp enough to cut glass—silenced him before he could speak. "Silas," she said, soft but iron underneath. A warning wrapped in silk. "Forgive him," she told the room. "He is still in mourning. Leave us. *Per favore.*"

Even wolves listened when Alessia Vassallo told them to. One by one, they filed out.

Only August stayed. He didn't look at me with anger this time, not even disappointment. Just shock, raw and open, like he couldn't believe what he'd heard. Hell, neither could I.

"*Amore mio,*" my mother's voice, low, heavy with meaning. *What are you doing?*

I exhaled slow, forcing resolve into my words. "I only came back for the funeral. I'm not here to take Cesare's place."

Her brow tightened, her mouth hardening into something between a plea and a threat. "You are the eldest. Do you expect Augustus to take it from you? He is your little brother." The tenderness drained from her voice, replaced with steel. "You were always meant to return. Always. What would your papà say, if he were here?"

The question landed like a blade. If Cesare were here, he'd tell me to stop whining and bleed like a man for the family. He'd call weakness by its name and break me until I wore the crown gladly.

I glanced at August, half-hoping, half-daring him to take it from me. *Say something. Say you want it. Save me from this.* But his lips only twitched, silence anchoring him in place.

"It's time to come home," my mother said, rising, Arnaldo stepping forward to steady her. "The family needs you. Remember—you are a Vassallo."

Her words clung like chains, and I almost smiled at the irony. Remember. As though I'd ever been allowed to forget.

I shoved back from the table, the chair scraping against the polished floor loud enough to make them all flinch. *Good.* Let them hear it, let them feel a fraction of what was boiling in my chest. I didn't wait for my mother's protests, or for August's silence to calcify into something uglier—I just left, the weight of their eyes burning holes in my back as I pushed through the heavy doors and into the corridor.

The air outside the room was no lighter. It clung, stale and suffocating. I loosened my tie, fingers shaking with frustration, and paced down the hall until the muffled voices behind me dulled to nothing. My breath was ragged, shallow. I wanted to rip the suit off, peel this skin they'd forced me back into, and run. But run where? How far can you really get when your blood drags you back like a leash?

"Silas."

Arnaldo's voice carried easily in the silence. Not sharp, not loud, but firm enough to freeze me mid-step. I turned, finding him leaning against the wall just beyond the doorway. He hadn't chased me—Arnaldo never chased—but he'd followed, steady and deliberate, like a shadow you couldn't shake.

"What?" My voice was rougher than I meant it to be, too raw, like the anger was still chewing through me from the inside.

He studied me with that same unreadable look he'd worn since I was a boy. Never judgment, never affection. Just...

assessment. His arms folded over his chest, the cuff of his suit pulled tight around his forearm, the picture of composure in contrast to the storm ripping me apart.

"You can't storm out every time the world presses its weight on you," he said finally, his tone flat, almost conversational. "You'll run out of doors to slam."

What was he? A fuckin' philosopher now.

A bitter laugh clawed its way out of me. "So what then? I should just sit there? Smile? Pretend I want this life again, like it's a jacket I can slip back into without choking on it?"

Arnaldo tilted his head slightly, eyes narrowing. "I'm not saying you have to want it. But refusing it doesn't make it vanish. It just makes you look weaker than they already think you are."

The words cut, because they were true. And he knew it.

I pressed my tongue against my cheek, forcing a smirk that didn't reach my eyes. "So what—you want me to embrace it? Become Cesare all over again?"

His gaze softened—not much, but enough to notice. "No," he said. "I want you to remember you're not him. You never were."

For a moment, the hallway felt too still. His words lingered like smoke, heavy and impossible to wave away. My chest tightened, not with anger this time, but something I didn't want to name.

I swallowed hard, dragging my eyes away from his. "Then what the hell am I supposed to be?"

Arnaldo didn't answer. He just pushed off the wall, straightened his jacket, and walked past me back toward the room, leaving me with nothing but silence and the echo of a question that had no answer.

Chapter Thirteen

Philetos

I had never seen an Eudaimon before. I'd heard the tales, of course, murmured in the agora and etched into temple walls by artisans who had known the brush of a divine hand. I had seen them in mosaics, in faded pigments on clay, in the fluted marble of the Parthenon itself—winged figures draped in celestial light, as distant from us as stars from the earth. But I had never imagined I would witness one up close, not until that fateful afternoon when I found myself seated upon the sun-warmed steps of the temple, the weight of the world slipping from my shoulders, leaving only the quiet hum of inspiration beneath my skin.

The words came unbidden, a song carried on a wind I could not feel, plucking the strings of my lyre as if they had known the melody long before I did. It was not until later, when the echoes of my voice faded into the open air, that I sensed him. I had not known he was there, watching. His presence settled around me, familiar yet unfathomable, like the whisper of an ancient story at the edge of memory. And then, as if summoned from the heart of a dream, I saw him.

His hair, dark as the void between stars, framed a face that seemed carved from shadow and light, and his wings—those raven-like wings—glistened with a faint blue hue, the golden hour catching on their edges as though the sky itself bent to his beauty. I could not tear my gaze away. He was the embodiment of something more than beauty, something divine, an ideal given form. And in that moment, I knew. This was what it felt like to find one's muse. This was the surge that poets spoke of, the fire beneath the skin, the feeling that the gods themselves had reached down to stir your soul into creation.

My mother used to say I was kissed by the Theion, blessed with a voice and a gift for spinning stories from the ether. She would smile as I played, her eyes soft with belief, telling me that I would bring forth songs the gods themselves would weep to hear. But my father... ah, my father. He saw only a boy wasting his life, charming crowds with words that would fade like the morning dew, urging me to stand with the Athenian army, to forge my legacy with a sword, not a lyre. He said my gifts would wither, my voice grow hollow with time. But now, with an Eudaimon standing before me, surely my destiny lay elsewhere—in art, in beauty, in the weaving of something timeless.

His name, I learned later, was Zayd. The raven-winged Eudaimon who had become the center of my world.

"If you are to play for the King, you must present yourself with dignity," he said one day, his voice smooth as the wind rustling through olive branches. "Stand as though the weight of every note matters. Let the world see you as more than just a poet."

To have an Eudaimon at my side was blessing enough, but to perform before Pericles himself? It was almost too much to fathom.

"And it will not be just Pericles," Zayd added, leaning against one of the marble pillars, his arms folded in casual elegance. "The archons will be there, the aristocrats—the eyes of Athens upon you."

The weight of it all pressed down on me then, a knot forming in my chest. I laid my quill down on the table, the ink drying as swiftly as my thoughts stilled. "What if... what if I make a fool of myself? What if they find me lacking?" I glanced at the half-finished scroll, the words frozen in time. "I am no Sophocles. No Aristophanes. I am just—"

"You are just what, Philetos of Aristodemos?" Zayd's lips curved into a gentle smile, his head tilting as he studied me. "Philetos the Nightingale?" His voice held a playfulness, a kindness that sent my heart fluttering like the wings of a startled bird.

"I am just... yes," I whispered, the words small, insignificant compared to the weight of his gaze.

"What you feel now, capture it," he said, his voice low, intimate, as though it carried the wisdom of the stars. "Let your soul spill onto the page. There is nothing more powerful than the truth of emotion, nothing more beautiful than the vulnerability of the heart laid bare in art. And no one, no king or commoner, can resist the way the soul manifests through your voice."

The beat of my heart was loud in my ears, drowning out the rest of the world. How could one such as him—a creature of divine purpose—see me, a mere mortal, with such light in his eyes? I was no fool; I knew the Eudaimons were meant to inspire, to bring joy and muse to those lucky enough to glimpse them. But there was something different here, something that bound me to him in a way I could not yet understand.

Zayd was no longer just my muse. He was everything. And I... I was a man ensnared, enthralled, obsessed.

There came a moment, as there always does, when I could no longer contain the longing that had grown like ivy around my heart. Only a fool would dare to romanticize the divine, to believe they could reach for something so far beyond their grasp. But I had always been a fool for beauty, and so I reached.

"Zayd," I whispered, my voice trembling as my hand drifted over his thigh. The warmth of his body beneath my fingertips felt like a tether to something far beyond the mortal coil, something sacred. He sat beside me, close enough that the scent of him—earth and air, something unnamable yet irresistible—filled my lungs. I leaned into him, desperate for closeness, for a taste of divinity, but he recoiled, ever so slightly, instinctively, as though even proximity to me was dangerous. His name left my lips like a prayer I was too fearful to finish.

"Philetos," he murmured, his voice so soft I nearly lost it to the night air. His brows knit together, a frown pulling at the corners of his mouth, but there was no rejection in his eyes—only confusion, conflict, as though he stood at the edge of a cliff and couldn't decide whether to leap or retreat.

"Please forgive me," I breathed, closing the space between us. I couldn't stop myself. The need had taken hold, a hunger I had long denied now burning too brightly to extinguish. My lips found his, tentative at first, testing the boundary between us. I had to know how he tasted, how it felt to touch the divine, to claim what mortals had deemed unattainable. If I never did, how could I ever live with myself? Even if it meant the Theion would strip me of their favor, of him.

But he didn't pull away. He froze beneath my kiss, caught in the same storm that had swallowed me whole. His breath hitched, his chest rising and falling as though the very air between us had become too thick, too charged with what we dared to feel.

"I-I'm sorry," I stammered, finally pulling back, fear gripping my heart. *What had I done?*

Then, before I could fully retreat, his hand found my face, cradling my jaw as if it were the most precious thing he'd ever held. He pulled me back to him, his lips pressing against mine, answering the question I had been too terrified to ask. There was no hesitation this time, no restraint—only the fierce pull of longing, of curiosity, of something deeper and unyielding.

Time unraveled around us, seconds slipping into minutes, minutes into something immeasurable. We kissed, over and over, as though we were learning the language of one another, our tongues meeting with a hunger that had long been denied but never forgotten. I hadn't intended for it to go further—this, I thought, would be enough. But the tide between us had shifted, and neither of us seemed willing, or able, to stop it.

I found myself straddling him, my legs laying to rest on either side of his thighs, our bodies pressed so close that I could feel every beat of his heart, every shuddered breath he took. My hand, trembling yet determined, found both of our hardened lengths, stroking us together, pulling from us sounds of pleasure that felt like they belonged to someone else, someone far removed from the men we had been moments ago. My other hand tangled in his dark, silken hair, pulling him closer, urging him deeper. Our tongues danced, desperate, as though we had been starving for this—for each other—our entire existence.

The air around us was thick with the scent of our arousal, the mingling of sweat and lust and the raw, aching need that pulsed between us. Our moans filled the room, echoing off the stone walls like sacred hymns offered up to a god who had turned away. It was beautiful. This—this is what it must feel like to truly be touched by the divine.

We moved through the night, the boundaries between us dissolving as we pushed further, deeper, until our bodies became one. There was no more Philetos, no more Zayd—just the heat of our skin, the rhythm of our bodies, the unspoken vows that passed between us in every breath, every thrust. My legs tightened around his waist as he looked down at me, his eyes dark and endless, the weight of the universe in his gaze. My fingers dug into his back, careful to avoid the ethereal wings that arched behind him, black as night, a reminder of the power he carried, the power I had dared to touch.

He moved within me, his hips a slow, steady rhythm, and I felt myself dissolve beneath him, into him. He was all consuming, and I was lost, willing to be lost, willing to give up everything I had ever known for this, for him.

All good things come to an end, or so it seems, as though the gods themselves delight in reminding us that the heights we reach are never ours to keep. Icarus flew, and so did I, soaring toward a light I had no right to touch, knowing full well that to fall from such a place would mean an end that no mortal—or even Daimon—could escape. We knew what we were doing, Zayd and I. We spoke of it often enough in the quiet hours of the night, when the stars blinked down on us like watchful eyes, indifferent to our whispered confessions. We told ourselves, time and time again, that we should pull away, sever whatever this was before it became our undoing. But words, it seems, have little power when weighed against the force of desire. Our promises were fleeting, as ephemeral as the breeze that stirred the leaves around us, and just as easily forgotten.

It was not long before the Theion came for me. Fate, that relentless tide, had decided that our love was not meant to be, and who among the living or divine can stand against such a decree? It came as a sickness, creeping into my body like a shadow I could not shake. There was no warning, no gradual descent into illness—only the swift, unmistakable hand of the gods. A dark mark burned into the side of my neck, the shape of a handprint, as if some unseen force had caressed me in the night. I did not feel it. It was only when another pointed it out to me that I knew. The gods had made their message clear: this was no mortal affliction. This was their will. They wanted the world to know that I was not dying by mere chance, but by their decree.

The fever came next, a searing heat that consumed me from within. My skin blistered, my body betrayed me with every breath, and soon the bile came, relentless and bitter, burning its way through me as if the very essence of my life was being pulled from my veins. I was dying. There was no question in my mind, no doubt in Zayd's. He tried, of course—how could he not? He who had once healed with a touch, whose divine gifts had been his birthright. He called upon the Aither, but they had cut him off, severed his connection to the very power that had once flowed through him. His magic faltered, useless in the face of the gods' wrath, and I could see the despair in his eyes as he realized there was nothing he could do.

In my final hours, a strange peace settled over me, a numbness that spread through my body like a balm. They say there is calm before the end, and perhaps that was what I felt—a brief reprieve from the agony that had wracked me for days. I could still see him beside me, though my vision had blurred, his figure hazy as if I were already halfway between life and death. Zayd never left me, not once. Even as he cursed the Theion, his voice hoarse and broken from the endless weeping, he remained at my side. His eyes, red and swollen, held a grief that made him look all the more beautiful—more mortal. In those moments, I wondered if Daimons were capable of feeling more than we ever imagined, if they truly were the bridge between divinity and humanity.

"I hope you know," I rasped, my voice weak, "I do not regret any of this." It was the truth, clearer to me in those final moments than it had ever been before. "If it were possible, and I was given the chance to live it all over again, I would. I would seize that opportunity every time, even if it meant death for me. I would not care, because I would have you. Even just a glimpse of this..." My voice faltered as his gaze lifted to meet mine, his lips trembling as he fought to hold back the sobs that threatened to break him apart. Tears streaked his skin, and he looked at me with a kind of desperation that made my heart ache.

"Any death is worth just a fraction of your love," I whispered, knowing that my words could never truly capture the depth of what I felt. Like a moth to a flame, I had been drawn to him, even knowing that I was destined to burn. And now, in the final moments of my life, I knew it had all been worth it.

"I love you," I breathed, the words barely audible.

"I love you," he said, his voice cracking as he rose from the side of the bed to press his lips to my forehead. I could feel the strain in him, the barely contained anger that simmered beneath the surface, threatening to consume him. "I will always love you," he vowed, the words heavy with the weight of a promise I feared he could never truly keep.

As I took my last breath, I prayed—if prayers still meant anything—that he would not let the grief devour him, that in time, he would find love again, even if it was not with me.

Silas

Consciousness crept back to me, and my fingers instinctively curled into the sheets, searching for the warmth of him beside me. "Zayd," I murmured, the name a soft plea on my lips. My voice was thick with the remnants of sleep, or perhaps death—I could not tell. All I knew was that I remembered.

I remembered everything.

Chapter Fourteen

Zayd

"Zayd."

He said my name with a weight that pulled me from the stillness of Khaos, not a whisper or a soft murmur in sleep, but a plea—ancient, familiar, one I had not heard for lifetimes but had known too well in the past. The expression painted on his face, the way his brows knitted, the subtle parting of his lips, the tension in his jaw—I had memorized it once, carved it into the deepest reaches of my mind and heart, etching the contours of his soul into my own.

Philetos.

I had watched him sleep before, as I always did, silently observing from the shadows between worlds, watching as visions played behind his closed eyelids. But this time was different. No warning, no whisper from the Theion, could have prepared me for this moment.

"Zayd."

His voice again, breaking through the haze as he stirred, sitting up on the bed, his eyes searching the room, as though he sensed me there, lingering just out of reach. But he couldn't see me, not yet. I stepped out from the Khaos, letting myself slip into the mortal realm, taking my place by his side. He did not flinch, did not look surprised.

"Silas," I said softly, the name hanging in the air between us.

His gaze met mine, dark and filled with something I had not seen in him since Philetos drew his last breath in my arms. "I... I remember," he whispered, his voice thick, jaw tightening as he swallowed. "I remember everything, *agapi mou*." The words were laced with an accent long forgotten by this world, but all too familiar to me. Without hesitation, he reached for me, pulling me down onto the bed, arms wrapping tightly around me as though centuries had passed since our last embrace. And they had.

"Philetos?" My voice trembled, another crack in the stoic facade I had worn for millennia. I knelt beside him, hands trembling as they cupped his face, studying the features I had lost and found again, both foreign and achingly familiar. None of his past incarnations had ever remembered. Was this because the tether had snapped, because his cycle was ending?

"Philetos." The name escaped me again, unbidden, a tear spilling over as I pressed my forehead to his. The Theion had given him back to me, yet in their cruelty, they would soon take him away again.

He kissed me then, his lips meeting mine with a desperation I had not felt in ages, as though time itself bent beneath the weight of that moment. I held him as if I could stop it all—stop fate, stop the inevitable. But we both knew I could not.

"Ever since we met outside my bar.." he began, his breath warm against my skin, his forehead resting against mine. "I've had dreams, dreams that weren't just dreams. They felt real—like memories. And now, I realize they were." His words faltered, and he let out a soft chuckle, the sound strained. "I'll be honest, Zayd. My head is so fucked right now." His laugh turned bitter, almost self-deprecating. "I have all these memories, all these feelings, but I'm still me—Silas. I don't know how to explain it—"

"You don't need to." I cut him off gently, pressing a kiss to his cheek, then the other, grounding myself in the present, in him. "What matters is that we are here, together."

He laughed again, softer this time, pulling back just enough to meet my gaze. His eyes gleamed with that familiar mischief, that charm that was uniquely Silas. "Were you watching me sleep?" he asked, teasing, his hands moving to my waist. "You came the moment I called your name."

"Well," I began, unable to suppress the small smile tugging at my lips. "There's only so much one can do in a day—especially when sleep is unnecessary." I hesitated, unwilling to admit the truth: I had watched him out of fear, the unbearable thought that if I turned away for even a moment, he might be lost to me forever. The warnings of the Theion echoing in my mind.

He cocked his head, his grin widening, eyes darkening with playful intent. "And what else have you watched me do?" His voice dropped, a hand slipping from my waist to rest against my back.

"I have seen more than I should have," I confessed, warmth flooding my cheeks at the memories. Through Philetos' many lives, I had watched him love, watched him succumb to lust, desire, passion that did not belong to me. I had endured it all in silence, knowing it was not my place to intervene.

"Hm," he mused, his lips brushing against the skin of my neck. "I'm sorry I forgot you."

"It was never your fault."

He kissed my neck again, his breath mingling with mine as he held me tighter. "But you never forgot me, even after millennia. You waited for me—always. So loyal, so dedicated. It's... sweet." His tone was teasing, but there was a tenderness in it that nearly broke me.

"I meant it, Philetos," I whispered, my voice barely audible. "I meant it when I said I would always love you."

"Silas," he corrected softly, pulling back to meet my gaze again. "I may have Philetos' memories, but I'm not him—not entirely."

He was right, of course. He was Silas now, shaped by this life, molded by experiences internal and external. His memories and emotions of Philetos were fragments, slowly being woven into the man he had become, but still—he was Philetos, too, and I could not let go of that.

"Silas," I breathed, my voice breaking as his teeth grazed my neck, the sensation grounding me in the present moment.

He smiled against my skin, lifting his gaze to meet mine once more. "How is it that you've managed to stay as beautiful as you were all those years ago? It's not fair to us humans."

"I am not the same," I whispered, the weight of being forsaken pressing down on me. I felt myself fade, dulling ever since the Theion stripped me of my powers, my wings. "You, though, at least this time—you're nearly the same as when we first met."

"Nearly?" He smirked, pulling me closer. "Well, I hope this form still pleases you, even if it's a little different. I don't want you to grow tired of looking at me."

The laugh escaped me before I could stop it. "I could never grow tired of you, Silas," I said softly, brushing a hand against his cheek. "Your form doesn't matter. Only that you are you."

As if I could ever tire of his appearance, his voice, the very essence of his soul. He makes the world itself feel pale, a dull imitation of life, as though everything fades in his absence. When he's not near, it's as if the colors drain from the sky, the air grows still and silent, and I am left wandering through a hollow expanse, waiting—always waiting—for the moment his light returns, and with it, the world is reborn in vibrant splendor.

His hand pressed gently to my cheek, a soft warmth that belied the intensity of what was to come, and yet it was that very softness that drew me in, made me press into the kiss with a fervor I hadn't known in centuries. The taste of him stirred something deep within me, something I had kept locked away for far too long. He pulled me into his lap, the heat of his body melding against mine, forcing me to straddle him as his fingers tangled in my hair, tugging just enough to expose the vulnerable line of my throat. His tongue grazed over my throat, slow and deliberate, as I drew in a sharp breath, the air between us thick with unsaid desire.

"Do you want me to fuck you?" His voice, low and husky, sent a shiver through me, his hand sliding up my thigh, inching closer, teasingly close to the hardness that had already begun to strain against my pants.

"Can't you tell?" My voice, though composed, wavered with the weight of my need as I guided his hand to the aching bulge, the evidence of my want for him.

He gave me a knowing squeeze, a fleeting moment of pressure before his hand retreated, wrapping firmly around my waist. In one fluid motion, he lifted me, his strength effortless, and laid me onto the bed. Silas knelt between my legs, his gaze never leaving mine as he pulled off his shirt, the muscles of his torso rippling beneath smooth, olive skin. Every movement of his was effortless, natural, like a predator knowing the exact moment to strike, and yet there was no malice in it—only hunger, only want.

He was devastatingly beautiful without even trying, the kind of beauty that draws the world around it into a state of reverence.

His fingers worked deftly, undoing the buttons of my pants, freeing my cock into the cool air of the room. Arousal already gleamed at the tip, and as I lifted my hips to help him rid me of my clothes, my hands fumbled at the buttons of my shirt. His hand rested on my thigh, fingers digging into the flesh with a possessive grip as he leaned down, his other hand wrapping around the base of my length.

"Has anyone ever told you how hot you look from this angle?" His voice was a sultry rasp, and when his gaze flicked up to meet mine, those dark, copper eyes held me captive, searching my face for every tremor of pleasure as his tongue trailed along the underside of my shaft.

A groan escaped my lips, my head falling back into the pillow, the sensation overwhelming, like being devoured whole and remade in his heat.

"N-No," I managed, my breath coming out in a ragged whisper.

"That's a shame," he purred, his voice dark and teasing. "Just means I'll have to make sure you know how deserving you are of being worshiped." His mouth engulfed me, taking me in, inch by inch, the warmth of his lips, the press of his tongue, drawing a sharp, uncontrollable gasp from my chest. My fingers found their way into his hair, tangling in the strands as I matched the rhythm of his movements.

"Silas," I moaned, his name a plea on my lips, my body trembling beneath him.

It was hard to believe this was happening again, that the man before me was not just Silas, but Philetos, the soul I had loved across lifetimes brought back to me. The joy of it was almost unbearable, but with it came the knowledge that this, too, was fleeting—that the cruelty of fate would take him from me again. And I knew that when it did, the loss would tear through me like it had the first time.

Silas pulled back, his mouth releasing me, leaving my cock swollen, aching for more. His gaze never wavered, and as he brought a finger to his lips, wetting it with the slide of his tongue, the moment seemed to slow, a warm anticipation growing deep within my groin. He pressed the finger against my entrance, teasing, and then slowly he was inside me, his mouth returning to my cock, his lips and tongue working me with the same unrelenting intensity.

I gave myself over to him completely, my body yielding as he pushed deeper, one finger then another, stretching me in slow, measured strokes. The pleasure built steadily, relentlessly, until I could no longer hold back, my body seizing in his grip, my breath hitching as I cried out his name. My release came in a blinding wave, my fingers tightening in his hair, the sheets bunched beneath my other hand as my orgasm surged through me, a pulsing, overwhelming sensation that left me breathless.

Silas' throat constricted as he swallowed, his fingers still working inside me, coaxing every last shudder from my body.

When he lifted his head, his lips glistened, and he wiped his chin with the back of his hand, his fingers still moving within me, teasing, until I was nearly undone again.

"Are you ready for me, love?" His voice was low, rough with desire, his eyes dark and hungry as they met mine. He leaned down, his tongue flicking over the tip of my cock, tasting the remnants of my release.

I could only nod, the words lost to me, as I gazed up at him, utterly at his mercy, knowing that in this moment, I would give him anything he asked of me.

Silas' gaze lingered on me, heavy with hunger braided through tenderness, his breath shallow as he eased the waistband of his sweatpants lower. The motion was slow, deliberate, as though savoring each heartbeat before the inevitable closeness. His cock, thick and hard, brushed against me, the heat of his skin igniting something primal within my chest. And yet I remained still—always too still—in the presence of him, of something that felt sacred, something I should not dare touch, though I ached to be touched by it.

"Don't tease me," I whispered, though the words trembled. My legs parted further, the silent confession of what I could not voice: *I needed him.*

But instead of giving in to my plea, his hand shifted away, reaching toward the drawer at the bedside. The sound of it sliding open was soft, intimate, yet it carried the gravity of anticipation. A bottle appeared in his grip, and when he tipped it, the cool sting of the lube spilled onto me. I gasped at the shock of it, the liquid sliding against my skin before his fingers spread it across me with slow, merciless patience.

The cold gave way to fire as his touch lingered, circling, pressing, teasing me where I burned to have the thick of him. Each trace was deliberate, worship and torment woven into one.

My hand guided him to where I wanted him most. "Silas," I breathed, the syllables breaking like a confession, "please." The tip of his cock pressed in, slick and insistent, just enough to remind me of the exquisite ache of desire unfulfilled.

A groan rumbled from deep in his chest, a sound that reverberated through me. "So impatient," he chided, though his voice was thick with need. "You've waited so long—what's another minute?" His chuckle, low and rich, was cut off by a moan as I pulled him in deeper, his eyes fluttering shut in pure, unguarded bliss.

I released him, allowing him to take over, to guide the rhythm of our union, and with each inch he claimed, my body fought to accommodate, to stretch and yield to him. The pressure was exquisite, the slow, deliberate way he filled me inch by inch until I could feel him in every part of me, as though he were not just inside my body but inside my soul, pressing against the very fabric of my being. His hips rocked gently at first, each movement sending a ripple through me, a shockwave of sensation that pooled low in my abdomen, curling tighter with every thrust.

Instinctively, I brought the back of my hand to my mouth, muffling the sounds that threatened to escape. I hadn't made a sound like this in so long.

Silas caught my wrist before I could stifle myself further. "No," he whispered, his voice carrying a softness that unraveled me. His fingers traced along my palm, parting my fingers with a deliberate tenderness as he pressed our hands against the bed. "Don't. That sound is divine—don't hide it from me."

The intimacy of that touch—of his fingers threading through mine, of his breath hot against my cheek—was more overwhelming than the pleasure itself. It was a quiet kind of reverence, a worship in the way he held me, in the way he moved. His thrusts picked up pace, slow becoming swift, gentle becoming relentless, and I could feel the build-up deep within me, a pressure that would soon snap and leave me undone.

His mouth found the curve of my shoulder, his teeth grazing my skin before sinking in—not to hurt, but to mark, to claim, as if I could ever belong to anyone but him. A sharp hiss escaped my lips, quickly swallowed by the low moan that followed. The primal sound of our bodies colliding filled the space, but it was the silence between, the unspoken communion of souls, that seemed louder, more deafening.

And then—*Philetos*. His name rose in my chest, choking me, but before I could exhale it, Silas' grip on me tightened. His teeth sank deeper into my shoulder, and I felt the moment his control broke, the moment he gave in completely to the waves of release, warmth spilling into me as he moaned against my skin. The fullness, the heat—it was too much, too perfect.

He released my hand and cupped my face, his touch so gentle it made my heart ache. His lips found mine, soft and tender, the kiss more than just an extension of our pleasure. It was a promise—one I wanted to believe in but couldn't. My arms wrapped around him, pulling him flush to me, as if I could hold him to me forever.

"I love you," he whispered, the words brushing against my lips.

"I love you too."

In that moment, we were eternal, lovers bound by something that transcended time. But deep down, I knew—this wasn't eternity. It was only the briefest glimpse of it. And as much as I wanted to drown in the feel of him, to let him consume me whole, I couldn't push away the weight of the truth any longer.

I needed to tell him.

Chapter Fifteen

Silas

The black wrought-iron gates groaned open like they hated every second of it, dragging the sound out as if to remind me I didn't belong here anymore. Two men in black stood on either side, armed and watchful, faceless pieces of furniture in my father's house. When the gates clanged shut behind us, the sound should've pressed on my chest, but it didn't. Not this time. Maybe because Zayd was in the passenger seat, calm as ever, like his presence alone bent gravity in my favor.

"How many times have I dragged you into this circus?" I asked, a grin twitching at my mouth, though the nerves hummed under it.

The Vassallo estate rose up in front of us, a marble tombstone disguised as a mansion. Ivy crawled the walls like it was trying to escape, pillars glared down with their perfect symmetry, and chandeliers sparkled behind arched glass as if money could bleach out the blood that built it.

"Not as many as you think," Zayd said, fingers brushing my jaw like he was grounding me. "Some lives your parents were already gone by the time we found each other. Other times.." His gaze shifted, distant. "They didn't accept us. We were both men then."

Something hollow turned in my chest. "Did we ever... marry? Or something close?"

His eyes carried something sharp, sorrow threaded with regret. "No. Never."

I could've pushed, but one look from him shut the thought down. So I smirked instead, leaning in for a quick kiss across the console. "Then I'll just have to make an honest man out of you this time." I pulled back with a grin. "Alright. Showtime."

We climbed out into the sun. The air here always felt heavier, soaked in expectation and ghosts. I'd spent years convincing myself this house didn't own me, but here I was again, walking back into its mouth.

The front door opened before we even touched it, polished wood gleaming like it wanted to blind me with its reflection. The smell hit first—expensive, suffocating. Power had a scent here: old wood, cold stone, polish hiding the rot underneath. Portraits stared down at us in the foyer: dead men with colder eyes, women wrapped in pearls like chains, children who already looked like ghosts.

"Mrs. Vassallo is in the conservatory," the staffer said, clipped, no warmth.

Of course she was. My mother's sanctuary. The only room Father never managed to sour, no matter how tight he clenched the rest of the house. If anything in here had ever been holy, it was hers.

We moved down the corridor, footsteps sharp against marble. The conservatory light spilled through the glass, softened by the greenery inside. I hesitated at the threshold.

And there she was. Kneeling in the dirt like her dress wasn't worth thousands, laughing—actually laughing—at something Arnaldo said as he crouched beside her, sleeves rolled up, careful hands brushing lavender stalks. The scent of it reached me even from here—sweet, sharp, a memory pressed into the air.

She looked... young. Or maybe not young, but alive in a way I hadn't seen since before Father carved the joy out of her. Before the mafia swallowed her whole. Now, with Cesare gone, something in her had unclenched. There was color in her again.

My fingers tapped against the glass, a restless beat that didn't belong in a place this soft. "Ma."

Arnaldo's head jerked up like I'd caught him doing something he shouldn't. Whatever ease had been in his eyes vanished, shutters slamming down in an instant, leaving only that stone-faced professionalism he wore like a second skin. But under it, I saw something else—guilt, or maybe just the awkwardness of being seen gentle in a house that didn't allow gentleness.

Her smile only widened, blooming like the flowers around her as she stood, brushing the soil from her hands.

"*Cucciolo.*" Her voice—light, warm, the kind of sound I'd spent my childhood chasing and my teenage years forgetting—wrapped around me. Then her gaze slid past me, to Zayd, and the air changed. It always did when her curiosity sharpened, like time leaned in to listen.

"Who is this handsome man?"

Zayd didn't move, didn't need to. He was calm, unreadable, but I could feel the question in his stare on my back: *Your move.*

And suddenly my throat was full of gravel. I'd always known myself. Always. My body, my hunger, the shape of what I wanted—never a mystery. But knowing and naming are two different monsters. Knowing is safe in your bones. Naming is setting it loose in the world, where everyone else can put their hands on it.

I never had to "come out." Legare doesn't give you the space for that—every breath is survival, every relationship just another leverage point waiting to be broken. There were no boyfriends, no lovers, just bodies and shadows. And if Cesare were still alive? He'd have married me off to some Legare daughter like a business deal in a dress. "*The name must grow,*" he would've said. "*Blood builds legacy.*"

My jaw tightened, but I forced the words out anyway. "This is Zayd Aristodemos."

That surname on my tongue felt like a betrayal and a prayer all at once. It rolled out of me, unbidden, causing my heart to stutter, as if the act of speaking it, of bringing it into this world, had suddenly made it real in ways it never had been before. I wanted to give him everything—my name, my life, this fucked-up legacy, whatever pieces were left to hand over. I reached for his hand, fingers weaving through his, grounding me, daring me.

"This is my boyfriend." My voice came out rough, stripped down, no mask to hide behind. "Thought it was time you finally met."

The words cracked something open in the room. Arnaldo shifted, and I caught the flicker across his face—understanding, maybe even sympathy. He didn't say a word, just muttered about work and slipped out. I didn't blame him. The second I walked through those gates, I'd wanted to leave, too.

Silence held for a beat. Heavy. Waiting.

But my mother didn't falter. Her eyes stayed soft—always soft, even after life had sharpened her on every edge it could find. "I am pleased to meet you, Zayd," she said, her voice steady, like this wasn't the bombshell it was. "I hope my son has been good to you."

"Of course," Zayd answered softly, giving her the steadiness I couldn't.

"Come," she said, gesturing toward the stone table at the conservatory's center, sunlight spilling across it. "Sit. Silas has never brought anyone home before."

We followed her to the table at the center of the conservatory, a slab of fossilized limestone and glass polished so clean I could see my own unintentional scowl in it. Sunlight spilled down from the vaulted ceiling, gilding everything in a glow that made the whole room look softer than it was. A table like this was meant for lazy breakfasts, for stories over wine, for family. Not for what we were about to do.

We sat. For a moment, it almost felt normal. My mother across from me, Zayd at my side, his hand brushing mine beneath the surface. A picture of domesticity so convincing I almost believed it. Almost.

The conversation started light, the kind of small talk you'd expect—how we met, what he liked about me, the polite laugh she gave when I muttered something about my winning personality. The kind of questions that should've been easy. They weren't. Every word from my mouth was a mask, a wall, keeping me from the shit I truly needed to say.

The real reason I was here clung to the edges of the conversation, waiting, gnawing at me until I couldn't hold it back any longer. "There's something else." My voice carried the weight I couldn't soften. "Legare."

Her smile faltered. Not much—she never let much slip—but enough. "There will be a target on your back if you leave completely," she said, the words like a scalpel. Clean. Sharp. "You know that, don't you?"

"I know." Bitter. Like blood on my tongue. "August can take Cesare's place. He deserves it more than I do."

August had always been loyal to Legare in ways I never could be. He was here, committed, willing to die for them if need be. I looked at Zayd then, the way his fingers pressed lightly into mine under the table, and I knew I couldn't give

Legare the same kind of loyalty. I couldn't promise it my bones. I wanted more. For him. For us.

But my mother didn't blink. "*Amore*, you already are the head. It was written in the will. It's already done. You stepping down would mean stepping down Vassallo as the head of Legare. It would be seen as weakness."

The weight of it pressed hard against my ribs. The Vassallo name had always been armor—shiny enough that no one dared test how thin it was. If I took it off, if I threw it aside, I'd be exposing all of us. Her. August. Zayd. And the Callaghans were already circling. Others would come. They always did.

"You wanted out because you wanted something of your own," she went on, her voice gentler now, carrying that note of grief she always tried to swallow. "So don't live in your father's shadow. Make Legare your own."

I wanted to laugh at that, at the absurdity of it. My own? Like repainting a coffin made it anything but a box for the dead. But the words stuck.

"Augustus isn't fit," she added, softer, darker. "He's... unwell."

I met her eyes, and the truth sat there, ugly and bare. I wasn't her first choice. I was just the lesser of two evils.

"Can I have time to think?"

"There is no time." The exhaustion in her voice wasn't just for me—it was for her, for all the years she'd already spent chained to this life. "Sometimes we don't get to choose. We do what we must to survive. Even if it means sacrificing ourselves."

She wasn't talking about me. Not really. She was talking about herself—her marriage, her years under Cesare's thumb, the life she endured so we could keep breathing. Now it was my turn.

Her gaze flicked to Zayd, then back to me. "We'll make this work. You have a week to settle your affairs. Then it's time. You were born for this, Silas."

Born for this. The words dug in like a brand, searing themselves into me. Not a promise. Not even a destiny. Just a curse I hadn't found the courage or enough reason to break.

The car was too quiet, the kind of quiet that doesn't let you breathe. The hum of the engine did nothing to fill it, nor did the monotonous roll of tires over asphalt. Silence had teeth tonight. Every word exchanged at the estate chewed its way through me on repeat, every look from my mother burrowed under my skin until it felt like I was suffocating in my own head.

And then Zayd spoke, his voice low, deliberate, slicing the quiet down the middle.

"There's something I need to tell you."

My hands tightened on the wheel, knuckles blanching. I didn't look at him. "This the part where you say it's too much? That you want out?" My tone was meant to be careless, but it came out brittle, already fractured. *Of course,* I thought. He'd seen the mess I lived in, the blood and shadow, so different from the beauty of Philetos—the soft light that once drew him in. I couldn't expect him to keep wading through this ugliness with me.

He released a soft exhale, one that seemed to carry the weight of the universe. "No." I could feel his gaze, burning, intense from where he sat beside me. "I... I don't know how to say this, Silas. That's why I haven't yet."

"Well," I muttered, forcing a humorless laugh, "now you've got me nervous." I jerked the wheel, pulling us off to the shoulder, gravel crunching under the tires as the headlights lit up nothing but empty highway. I threw the car in park, my pulse hammering harder than it should've. "Just spit it out, Zayd. I can take it."

"The Theion... the gods," he corrected himself, words delicate like they might shatter in the air. "They told me you're going to die soon. I don't know how or when, but... it's coming."

For a second, I almost laughed. Almost. But the sound curdled before it could leave my throat. Instead, I leaned back against the leather, a thin smile tugging at my mouth. "There's more isn't there? There's always more. Go on. Drop the rest."

Zayd hesitated, his hands gripping the edge of the seat, his fingers tense, pale against the darkness. "This is your last life, Silas. You won't come back after this."

I turned my head sharply, meeting his eyes, and the world seemed to tilt. Death? Sure. I'd stared that down enough times to know the taste of it. But final? No return, no second chances, no finding each other again in another decade, another century? That was something else entirely.

"So let me get this straight." My voice was dry, sharp enough to cut. "They let me remember everything—my first life, you—drag me through hell to claw it all back, just to kill me off after a few weeks? No reruns? No encore performance?" I barked a laugh, brittle and joyless. "That's fucking poetic."

Zayd swallowed, his throat tight. "If we want to simplify the ways of the Theion, then yes."

"That's bullshit, and you know it." I felt the frustration burning in my chest, raw and unbearable. "You're holding something else back. Don't look at me like that—*I know you.* I've always known you. So just fucking say it." My voice cracked at the end, betraying me, but I didn't care.

His eyes drifted to the windshield, staring at the empty road stretching out into the night. "It's my fault," he finally said, his voice breaking. "I'm the reason this life has been cut short. In every life, Silas, you have never lived past forty. Because of me. Because when we fall in love, when we're together... the Theion take you, again and again, as punishment. For repeating my mistakes. For wanting you, for being with you." His gaze fell, tears gathering at the corners of his eyes. "If I hadn't met you outside the bar... if I'd stayed away, you might've lived a full life before your final end. But I couldn't. I couldn't resist. And now—now it's happening again."

I just stared at him. Silent. Watching those tears slip down his face, helpless and raw. The same as that night centuries ago, when I died with him bent over me, begging. The same guilt, etched into him like a scar that never healed.

And here we were again.

The fury in me—the grief, the rage, the sharp-edged panic—it all slipped out of reach the moment I saw him breaking in front of me. I reached for his hand, tugging it into mine, and pressed my lips against his knuckles.

"If I'd known," I murmured, the words scraping low, soft, unforced. "If I could've remembered sooner, I'd have begged you to come. To pull me out. I don't give a damn about the gods, or their punishment, or the way they've twisted this game against us. All I care about is you. I'd die a million deaths if it bought me even an hour with you."

I lifted my other hand, brushing his cheek, chasing away the wetness there with my thumb. His face felt fragile under my touch, as if centuries of his guilt had worn him down to something breakable. "This isn't on you. Even if it were—it wouldn't change a thing. What matters is we're here. Together. If I die, I die knowing I had you. That's enough. Fuck the gods."

I leaned in, lips finding his with a gentleness I didn't know I still had in me. The taste of salt clung to him, the rawness of his grief pressed between us. I pulled back just enough to breathe against his mouth. "Zayd," I whispered, steady this time, "marry me."

His eyes flicked over me, searching, as if he needed to know I meant it. And then—"Yes." The word cracked, barely audible, but it was enough. Enough to quiet the world, enough to steady everything that had splintered inside me.

If this was my last life, then I'd live it with him. On my terms, not theirs. And as much as the thought made me sick, I knew what it meant—I'd need Legare. Their name, their empire, their protection. Not for me. For *us*.

I didn't say it out loud, but I had no intention of letting the gods decide when my story ended. If they thought they could take me away from him again, they were sorely mistaken.

Zayd leaned into me once more, pulling me out of my own head the way only he could—the way I liked it, the way I *needed* it. His lips brushed mine, soft at first, testing, then hungrier. My hand moved to the back of his neck, keeping him there, but before I could deepen it, I felt the strange shift of my seat as his body pressed closer to mine.

A low laugh slipped out of me. "What the hell are you doing?" The chair whined under me, slowly sliding back as if it had a mind of its own.

He laughed too, the sound breaking through the thick air that had been suffocating us since the estate. "This was hotter in my head," he admitted sheepishly, "but I was trying to make room for this—"

His words cut off as he swung himself over, straddling me with ease, his coat sliding off his shoulders, forgotten in the cramped space. His hands came up to frame my face, his palms warm against my skin, and then his mouth was on mine once more.

I groaned into the kiss, my fingers digging into his waist, grounding myself in the solid weight of him. Every thought, every ugly truth we'd just torn open, bled away under the press of his lips. He tasted like the promise of something worth dying for, like defiance dressed up as devotion.

Zayd ground down against me, rolling his hips with deliberate slowness, his ass pressing to the strain in my lap. His tongue slipped past my lips, teasing, insistent.

"Fuck..." I pulled back just enough to catch my breath, to drag the words out with a crooked smile. "Are you really that excited we're engaged?" My hands caught his hips, helping him move, dragging him harder against me.

His laugh was breathless, broken against my ear. "Have to celebrate somehow."

The heat between us was stifling, made worse by the narrow confines of the car. "Not much room here, love." The words were half-groan, half-laugh, but neither of us slowed.

His hand slipped down, undoing me, pulling me free, his fingers wrapping firm around my dick. "Are you really asking for distance right now?" he whispered, his mouth brushing the edge of my ear as his thumb smeared across the head, catching on the wet slit as he pressed firmly.

I bit down on a curse, my head pressing back against the leather seat. His body shifted above me, a quick movement, and then the heat of him was there too—his cock freed, pressed tight against mine. His hand wrapped around both of us, stroking, squeezing, forcing our precum to smear slick between us.

I watched him—watched the way his lips parted, soft and pink, as he let spit fall onto us. He worked it over our heads with long, slow strokes, dragging the mess down until it mixed with the heat of our skin.

"Shit," I muttered, unable to look away. I lifted my hand, pressing a finger into his mouth. His lips closed around it instantly, sucking like it was a cock, a moan humming low in his throat.

"Get it nice and wet, *vita mia*," I rasped, my voice rougher than I intended.

When I slid my finger free, a thin strand of spit stretched between us, snapping when I pulled away. My hands traced down the back of his pants, spreading him open with one hand, the other circling his hole in slow, deliberate strokes.

My finger slid into him, slow, deliberate, and his moan spilled out like music torn raw from his chest. His hand faltered on our cocks, the other braced against the headrest behind me like he hadn't already taken all of me before.

"Don't stop now," I whispered against the corner of his mouth, urging him on as he leaned closer, the heat of him swallowing me whole.

My nose dragged along his jaw, breathing him in, my lips grazing the shell of his ear before I caught his lobe gently between my teeth. "You've taken more from me," I murmured, pushing a second finger in, feeling him clench, stretch, yield.

Another moan—ragged, desperate—tore from his throat as his hand slipped from the headrest to curl around the back of my neck, pulling me up into him. Our mouths crashed together, breath against breath, tongues tangling in the kind of kiss that left no air between us, no thought beyond the desire in our bodies.

His hand found its rhythm again, stroking us both with a steady pace, slick and tight, each pull dragging a hiss from my throat. Our cocks slid together in his grip, wet and aching, smearing precum and spit across skin and knuckles.

The sound of it—our breaths harsh and uneven, the wet slide of his hand—filled the small space of the car, suffocating, intoxicating. The windows fogged, blurring the world outside until it was only us, only this heat, this hunger, pressing down and consuming everything else.

His hips rolled down against my hand, greedy for more, the tight heat of him pulling at my fingers like he was trying to drag me deeper. "Fuck, Zayd.." My voice broke rough in my throat as I worked him open, curling inside him just enough to hear the way his breath hitched, to feel his body melt and shudder against me.

"Silas," he gasped, my name spilling from him like a prayer, his forehead pressing to mine. His strokes quickened over our cocks.

I dragged my mouth across his cheek, down to his throat, sucking at the skin there until I left it marked. "You're perfect like this," I growled against him, sliding my third finger in, stretching him wider. "Falling apart in my hands."

He whimpered, his voice breaking as his hips jerked down harder onto my hand. His cock twitched against mine, his grip faltering only for a second before he pushed through, pumping us faster, desperate now.

"Good boy," I whispered, my free hand clutching at his ass, pulling him down tighter against me as I thrust my fingers into him, matching the rhythm of his strokes.

"Silas—I'm—" His voice broke as his head fell back, mouth parted, eyes half-lidded with the haze of it all.

I stole the words from his mouth with a kiss, swallowing his groan as his body trembled against mine. His hand worked us furiously now, our shafts pressed so tight together I could feel every throb of him against me, every pulse like a shared heartbeat.

"Cum with me," I rasped, biting his bottom lip hard enough to taste copper. "Now."

His whole body jerked as the first hot spurt of his release smeared between us, coating our cocks, his fist slipping messily through it as he came undone. The sound he made—wrecked, guttural—dragged me under with him. My own orgasm tore through me, thick and violent, spilling over his hand, over both of us, streaking across his stomach and mine as we ground together in the mess.

He collapsed against me, chest heaving, his cheek pressed to my shoulder, the faint tremors still running through him as my fingers slid free from his body.

I let out a low laugh, the sound rumbling against his cheek as I wrapped an arm around him, the other resting on the armrest. "Well," I murmured, pressing my lips to the crown of his head, "we've officially broken in the car as fiances."

He groaned against me, somewhere between exasperation and laughter, which only spurred me on.

"You know what that means, right?" I tipped my head down until my mouth brushed his ear, my voice dropping into a conspiratorial whisper. "There are... other places we'll have to take care of now. It's tradition."

Zayd actually laughed then, the sound muffled against my collarbone. "You're insufferable."

"Mm. And yet—here you are, still sitting on my lap and covered in cum," I shot back, grinning when his groan turned into another shaky laugh.

His hand slipped weakly down my chest, dragging our mess with it. "Theions, you're going to regret this when you try to drive tomorrow."

"Worth it," I said simply, softer now. My thumb brushed his jaw, tilting him up so I could kiss him again—slow, deep, lingering, tasting of salt and heat and something far too close to love.

When we pulled apart, I rested my forehead against his. "My love," I whispered, the words more like an oath than a tease. "We're going to ruin a lot more than just the upholstery."

Chapter Sixteen

Zayd

"So, is this official?" Ivy asked, her voice light as she dragged a cloth across the worn surface of the bar counter. The evening light streamed through the window, gilding the edges of the old wood, casting a soft glow on her face.

Silas glanced at her, his expression unreadable but for the subtle shift of his eyes.

"I'm only saying," she continued, her gaze flicking to me with a playful grin, "cause you've been around a lot, Zayd. Not necessarily inside the bar but..." Her eyes drifted meaningfully toward the stairs that led up to Silas' apartment, the space we shared away from everyone else.

I exhaled softly. That was the drawback, I suppose—getting a sense of normalcy by not slipping in and out of the Khaos to see him, but rather walking through the front door like any mortal might.

"Yes," Silas replied, his voice warm and edged with that knowing smile of his, the one that seemed to tug at the corners of the universe itself. "We are official."

"You're welcome," Ivy smirked, setting the cloth aside. "If I hadn't pushed you to show him around, you'd still be single and lonely."

Silas chuckled, the sound low and rich. "Oh, so this is all your doing now?"

Their laughter faded to the background for me. In the space between their voices, I felt it—a ripple in the fabric of the Khaos. A familiar presence stirring the air with its unmistakable energy. A Daimon lurked. Eryx.

"I have to head out," I murmured, rising from the barstool. My voice felt small against the pull of the Khaos, as though it belonged more to the ether than this world.

Before I could step away, Silas' hand shot out, his fingers wrapping around my forearm, firm but gentle, pulling me closer. His touch was warm—more than that. Alive. He reached up with his other hand, cupping the side of my face as he leaned in, pressing his lips to mine with a tenderness.

I froze for a moment, caught off guard by the simplicity of the gesture. It wasn't that the kiss itself surprised me—rather, it was the ease with which he did it. The last time we were together, in his past incarnation, we lived in the shadows, our affection hidden beneath layers of silence and societal shame. How foreign it felt now, to stand in the open, his lips brushing mine without fear. I had forgotten that the humans of this era had grown *slightly* more tolerant of love like this.

"Aw," Ivy cooed beside us as Silas pulled away, his eyes gleaming with amusement. "Don't make it weird," he laughed softly, releasing me. "I'll see you later."

"Bye, Zayd," Ivy teased, her voice laced with a mischievous edge.

I stepped into the street, the bar's warmth retreating behind me as the sun greeted my face. Its golden light seemed to hang between worlds, caught in the brief moment between day and dusk. And there, stepping out of the Khaos, was Eryx. His lips curved into a playful smile, his eyes catching mine with that ever-present gleam.

"You two are cute," he said, his voice smooth as ever, a ripple of mischief running beneath it.

"I hope that's not why you are here," I muttered, rolling my eyes as I fought back the flush that threatened to bloom. It was easier to deflect him than to let him see how his words hit their mark.

"Very cute." He folded his arms, a mock-seriousness settling over his features. "Almost as cute as the smile that's on your face right now."

It was then I noticed the lingering curve of my lips, followed by the flush that finally bloomed unbidden on my cheeks.

"Enough," I sighed, running a hand through my hair, "what is it, Eryx? You don't normally linger in the Khaos just to watch."

He grinned, a flicker of playfulness dancing behind his eyes. "Of course not. Only a stalker would do that." His teasing was light. "I just thought I'd give you a heads-up. Some men from Callaghan are on their way here."

My heart tightened, the familiar weight of dread settling in my chest. The Callaghans. I had known they'd try again, but so soon? And here again?

"They don't want Silas," Eryx said, as if reading my thoughts. His face sobered, his tone dropping. "They want you."

I laughed, a bitter sound escaping me as I raised a brow. "Me? Why?"

"They've been watching Silas. And now, they see you as his vulnerable spot."

I cast a glance back at the bar, where my world carried on without knowledge of the end creeping ever closer. My hand clenched, running through the strands of my hair. They couldn't hurt me, not truly. My body would heal faster than they could damage it, and even without my powers, I was still stronger than they could ever be. If I let them take me, perhaps I could draw them away, buy Silas some peace, even if only temporarily.

"I could deal with them," Eryx offered, a wicked gleam sparking to life once more. "Either stall them or end them. Maybe make it look like a deer jumped in front of their car, or have them slam into a truck. Just say the word, and I'll handle it."

His ease with interfering with mortals never ceased to amaze me. He, unburdened by the weight of being forsaken, still retained the freedom to act upon the mortal world in the ways of the Kakodaimon. He could weave his chaos into their lives with the blessing of the Theion, while I remained bound, shackled by my punishment.

"No," I said quietly, biting down on the inside of my lip. "I can handle this."

"Are you really going along with this?" His voice carried the weight of his amusement. "You, tied up like some helpless damsel?" His body now brushed up against mine as we lay crammed into the trunk of a car, my limbs bound and my face concealed beneath a bag. It was clear they believed they had caught me by surprise, thinking I was merely some mortal and mundane boyfriend of Silas.

"I won't lie," I replied, the bag muffling my voice slightly, "I'm also curious to see where this will lead."

Eryx's fingers trailed down my arm in the dimness, his touch both teasing and intimate. "You do look hot like this, though," he mused, his voice laced with dark humor as he pulled the hood off.

"Shut up," I murmured, but there was no true venom behind the words.

I was far more interested in how the Callaghans had found us. Silas had been hiding for five years, and yet they seemed to know everything, where he was and about me. I needed to find out how deep their knowledge ran.

"Eryx, do me a favor?"

"Anything for you, my Eudai," he replied, his voice lilting with an easy smile.

"Watch over Silas for me. Just until I take care of this."

"Consider it done,"

The car rolled to a stop, the sound of gravel crunching beneath the tires. There was murmured conversation outside, the shift of bodies against the vehicle. They were waiting for something. Or someone.

"Play nice with the mortals," he said before vanishing into the Khaos, leaving me alone with the weight of what's to come.

Soon after, another car approached, its tires dragging over the gravel, slower, heavier. The door slammed and additional footsteps came closer. I knew that voice.

Augustus.

The trunk creaked open, and I saw the flicker of surprise in his eyes—a momentary lapse of the bravado he was attempting to construct. His brow furrowed, not in rage but in mild disappointment, as though a simple mistake had been made, something as trivial as an overcooked meal or a misstep in a well-rehearsed dance. He looked at the man beside him, an unspoken reprimand passing between them.

Then, his gaze returned to me, sharp and assessing, like a hunter reassessing his prey. There was no hint of surprise in my expression, just indifference.

"I had thought," he began, his voice a low murmur, almost somber, "that you would be my salvation." His fingers worked at the cuff of his shirt, unbuttoning the fabric with a meticulousness that belied the gravity of his words. The sleeves rolled up slowly, as though he were preparing for some delicate task. "I thought they'd cut Silas loose if he were in love with a man. I thought it would save us—that by loving you, he would compromise his position as head, because the Vassallo control over Legare would end with him."

He paused, his eyes narrowing as if inspecting the seams of this plan he had once so fervently believed in. "But it hasn't changed anything," he continued, his voice softening with resignation, the weight of his words settling like dust on forgotten relics. "Our fates are still as they always were. Unmoved. Unaltered."

His gaze hardened then, as though the softness had been an indulgence he could no longer afford. "But now," he said, his voice growing sharper, "I found another use for you."

I understood then, even before he leaned in close enough for me to feel the heat of his breath against my ear. He didn't want to kill me, he wanted to use me as bait. His whisper was as soft as it was venomous. "We have a code," he murmured, his lips curling into a smile I could not see but felt like a blade. "We don't touch the wives of mafia members. But the Callaghans... well, they've become messy."

He believed that Silas would come running to save his lover and that he would get into a fit of rage, taking on more than he could on his own here. The death would seem solely the responsibility of the Callaghans.

Augustus straightened, his eyes now gleaming with a cold determination. One of the men handed him a phone, and with a careless gesture, he waved toward me. "Try to look scared," he said, his tone almost mocking. "Not... whatever this is."

I watched him, feeling a strange detachment from the scene unfolding. His words, the posturing, the threats—they washed over me like wind through an open field, stirring nothing within. I had enough of these childish games. This petty sibling rivalry, this unnecessary family drama.

With a single, effortless motion, I tugged at the bindings, snapping them as easily as brittle thread. The silence that followed was palpable, the briefest suspension of disbelief as I rose from the trunk, unhurried, my eyes fixed on him. Augustus' face shifted, a flicker of hesitation breaking through his facade just before my fist connected with his jaw.

I didn't strike him out of anger. There was no rage, no vengeance in the act—only necessity. His body hit the concrete with a dull thud, unconscious.

"Don't kill him, we need him alive!" one of the men shouted, their voices rising now in the midst of things.

I moved through them, each one falling with such ease that it felt almost grotesque, the way a god might crush a handful of insects without thought or care. It wasn't something to take pride in—this effortless dominance over mortals. If anything, it saddened me, this reminder of the distance that always stretched between us, a chasm they could never cross, no matter how hard they tried.

They were ants, and I was not their kind.

Stepping over the bodies, I made my way back to Augustus. Crouching low, I let my fingers press lightly against his neck, searching for that persistent pulse. Still breathing, thankfully.

What am I going to do with you?

If it were up to me, I'd whisk him away somewhere far from all of this. Somewhere he could escape the shadow that loomed over him. I had watched him grow up alongside Silas, watched as the resentment quietly festered. How he had worked tirelessly for Cesare's approval, while Silas seemed to earn that twisted affection so effortlessly. It wasn't just because Silas was the firstborn.

I was not so blind in my love for Silas that I couldn't see the darkness rooted deep within him—a seed planted by his father long ago. But it wasn't just Silas who carried Cesare's legacy. Augustus had that same darkness in him, though neither of them realized it. They were both more like their father than they would ever admit.

There was a growing parallel I couldn't ignore, a reflection between the two brothers and their father, much like the one I had begun to see between the Daimons and the Theion. Kakodaimons, Eudaimons—both had the potential for both fostering and ruin, regardless of their outward forms. Both straining to please the Theion, though they were nothing but mirrors of their maker and the title given.

With a sigh, I slid my arms under Augustus' thighs and back, lifting him easily from the concrete. If he had been anyone else, I would have ended him here, just as I had with the man who attacked us outside the gallery. The Theion no longer held any expectations over me. That was one small solace in my fall—I was free to be both Kakodaimon and Eudaimon now without hesitation.

I drove in silence, the hum of Augustus' car like a low dirge beneath the chaos still crackling in my chest. The motel rose before me, unremarkable, a faceless, sagging structure cloaked in the anonymity of peeling paint and neon light. It was the kind of place that whispered of desperation and secrecy, where the stories told in its walls were left unfinished, discarded, or forgotten. *Perfect*, I thought. A purgatory for the powerful to wake to the stench of their own mortality.

Augustus in the passenger seat remained unconscious, his head slumped at an awkward angle, the rhythm of his breath shallow but steady. He was a titan brought low, stripped of his symbols of power: no phone, no wallet, no name that held weight in this city. Just flesh and blood now, as breakable as anyone else. I carried him inside, my hands steady despite the heaviness of the moment, and laid him on the bed's sagging mattress. The room smelled faintly of mildew and cheap cigarettes.

The head came next. A grotesque trophy taken from one of his men, its lifeless features frozen in an expression I couldn't bring myself to meet for long. I placed it with precision on the bed beside him, a silent herald of the message I'd come to deliver. No note, no flourish. The message spoke in a language far older than words, one Augustus would understand the moment his eyes opened. A warning, unmistakable in its simplicity: I am not the prey here.

I stood for a moment, looking down at the tableau I had created, the scene dark and twisted beneath the dim, flickering light. The head seemed too still, too silent, its weight a tangible presence in the room. My chest tightened, not with regret, but with something darker—something I couldn't name.

I had crossed a threshold. Augustus would understand. Men like him always did. He would see this not as barbarism, but as strategy, an echo of the language he himself had chosen to speak. He would know, in that instant of waking, that this wasn't about vengeance or fury. It was about control. About power.

Chapter Seventeen

Silas

The study reeked of dust and paper, the kind of silence that didn't comfort but pressed down, thick and suffocating. I hadn't seen August since Zayd and I moved into the estate, and the absence clawed at me more than I wanted to admit. Stupid of me to think that coming back to this house—the one we grew up in—might patch what years of silence and resentment had shredded. Proximity doesn't fix anything. If anything, it makes the cracks more visible.

Arnaldo had said August disappears sometimes, vanishing into whatever poison he's taken to numb himself with. He always comes back within a day or two, he'd assured me. But that didn't lessen the weight in my chest. He's my brother, and we were like strangers caught in the same current, but helpless to reach one another. I had enough on my plate with lawyers, accountants, the ghosts of my father's legacy all clawing for a piece of me. The five years I spent away? Gone in a breath. Legare doesn't wait.

I leaned back in the chair, hair falling into my eyes no matter how many times I pushed it aside, staring at the numbers until they bled into one another. My jaw cracked on a yawn, exhaustion dragging me under just as a knock pulled me out.

"Excuse me," I muttered to the accountant, pushing off the chair with a sigh. Anything to get out of the monotony.

I was fucking bored.

One of the men, his face forgettable like most of the new recruits, nodded as I opened the door. "Augustus just arrived."

"I'm not a child. I do not need to be announced." Came a voice from behind him—familiar, sharp, and cold. There he was. My brother. My stranger. He stepped forward, gaze skimming over me, over the papers, over everything, without landing. "Seems you're settling in easily." The words weren't a compliment.

I leaned against the frame, folding my arms, feigning ease. "You of all people should know we don't get much of a say in how our lives go." I searched his face for something—resentment, recognition, anything. "Where have you been?"

But he didn't answer, didn't even acknowledge the question. "Madre told me you have a boyfriend living here with us now," he said instead, as though that was the only thing of interest. "When do I get to meet him?"

I sighed, pushing off the frame, stepping towards him. He wasn't looking at me, wasn't *really* looking at anything. I grabbed his jaw, tilting his face to the light. His pupils were blown wide. Too wide.

"What the fuck, Silas?" he spat, grabbing my wrist, his voice harsh. But I didn't let go, narrowing my eyes.

"Are you high?" My voice came out low, quiet, disappointment scraping against anger. My grip tightened. "We don't dip into that shit. We don't sell it, we don't touch it. You know better."

He rolled his eyes, muttering, "It's legal." But the words rang hollow.

I released him, stepping back. The space between us felt heavy, brittle. "For your sake, it better be."

The rules were carved into us, same as the name we carried. No drugs. No women. No children. We weren't some petty street gang running on chaos. Legare had limits. And he knew it.

Zayd appeared in the hallway, silent as always, but present, he had a way of knowing when I needed him. "Is this your brother?" he asked softly, resting a hand briefly on August's shoulder.

August went rigid at the touch, eyes flicking over to Zayd for the first time. His stare was cool, detached, but I saw the calculation there—measuring, dissecting, the way we'd been raised to do with strangers and enemies alike.

"August, this is Zayd," I said, watching the flicker of something unreadable cross his face. "Zayd, August."

Zayd extended his hand, polite, expression smoothed over into something unreadable of his own. "It's nice to meet you."

For a moment, August just stared, like he was weighing whether to even bother. Then he smiled, the kind of smile that doesn't reach the eyes, and shook Zayd's hand. "Likewise," he said, his tone light but hollow. "Alessia mentioned you'd be staying with us." He glanced at me then, the smile shifting into something sharper. "I was just coming to see my brother, thinking the three of us could grab a drink. Get to know each other a bit better. Catch up, since we'll be under the same roof. It doesn't make sense for us to be strangers."

His eyes locked with mine at that last word—strangers. A reminder. A rebuke. Maybe both.

I exhaled slowly, reading between the cracks of his act. He was trying, in his own crooked way. Or maybe testing me, seeing if I'd take the olive branch or break it in half. Either way, it was more than we'd had in years.

"I'd like that," I said finally, my voice lower, softer than I meant it to be. A truce, or at least the closest thing we could manage. Maybe it wouldn't fix anything. But if it dulled the sharp edges between us, even a little, I'd take it.

"How much do you trust your brother?" Zayd's voice was a whisper, low enough that only the space between us could hear. His eyes were fixed on August's retreating form.

Saying I trusted August at all was a stretch. I trusted that he would do what was right by Legare. That's it.

"A decent bit," I muttered anyway, watching that same figure dissolve into the shadows of the estate. "He's a good kid. Just cracked in places he shouldn't have been. Courtesy of him." My jaw tightened at the thought of our father, the ghost of Cesare still curling around every corner of this house. "We all are, one way or another."

I slid my arms around Zayd's waist, pulling him against me, grounding myself in his warmth. "Why? What's rattling around in that head of yours?"

"He seems... off." Zayd's brow furrowed, his body stiff against mine.

I couldn't help it—the laugh slipped out, low and bitter, like it had been waiting in my chest. "That's because you don't know him. He's always off. That's August in a nutshell. He lives half a step outside of reality—like he's in some locked room the rest of us don't have the key to."

I leaned in, kissed him, soft but deliberate, a reminder that not everything had to spiral into suspicion and ghosts.

Zayd kissed me back, lips yielding, but I could feel the weight he was carrying, the storm brewing behind his calm. "I suppose," he breathed, but his tone betrayed him.

"There's something you're not saying."

He pulled back just enough for me to see the tightness in his face, the caution in the way his eyes searched mine. "What do you mean?" His voice was careful, but we both knew better.

I traced my fingers along the curve of his neck, finding the small betrayals he couldn't mask. "You get tense right here,"

I murmured, brushing the spot where his pulse ticked faster. My hand slid up, resting against the sharp line of his jaw. "And you clench here." I pressed lightly, feeling the muscles twitch beneath my fingers. "So tell me—what is it you're holding back?"

His hand came up, wrapping around my wrist, gentle but firm, like he could stop me with touch alone. "It's nothing," he said finally, voice quiet, too quiet. "I'm just... paranoid. You know why." His eyes gave him away. That flicker I knew too well: fear, not for himself, but for me. Always for me.

Ever since I told him I was stepping back into Legare, he'd been like this—strung tight, always watching the corners, scanning the dark like something was waiting there to take me. I'd tried to explain it, that staying away left me more exposed, that here, of all places, was safer. The fortress of Vassallo. But logic never quieted his heart. I could see the way it clenched every time the air shifted, the way it beat harder when the world felt too close.

"Stop worrying, *vita mia*," I murmured, tilting his chin so he'd meet my eyes. I kissed him, slow, meant to loosen the knots in his chest. "This place is a damned fortress. Nothing's getting in."

The smile he gave me barely counted, just a faint curve at the edge of his lips—and it gutted me. How could someone like him, all light, always look so close to breaking? "It's cute how much you care," I tried, forcing the tease, slipping humor into the cracks.

He pressed his lips flat, unimpressed. Dissatisfaction dressed as silence. I kissed the corner of his mouth, soft, coaxing. "Don't pout," I added with a laugh, though I knew it was more than pouting.

"I don't pout."

"Fine. Don't brood then." The joke hung between us, lighter than what it tried to cover.

He leaned back, just enough to make space, to breathe. "Finish your work," he said softly, but I heard it—the plea beneath. "So we can be together."

"I'm working on it," I replied, feeling the weight of all the unfinished things between us, between me and this life I was stepping back into. "I shouldn't be too much longer."

And then—his smile. Small, quiet, enough to knock the air out of me anyway. It always did. There aren't words for him, not really. Nothing to explain how someone so perfect could sit here with me, or how every piece of him seemed carved from light even when shadows clung to him. That's what pulled me to him, life after life. That light. Even now, when he carried gloom like armor, weighed down by gods and punishments I never asked him to bear. He once told me I was the Theion's most beautiful creation—said it like fact, like gospel—but he couldn't have been more wrong. It was him. Always him. And all I wanted was to take that weight off his shoulders, strip him down to who he was meant to be—unburdened, unbroken, free.

"You know where to find me," he said, stepping away, carrying a piece of me with him like he always did.

Cuore mio.

"August and I haven't spent time like this in over five years," I muttered, softer than I meant to, as I began working the buttons of my shirt. The fabric clung to me, stiff and suffocating, and I silently cursed whatever bastard first decided that wealth meant choking yourself to death in overpriced layers. Whoever they were, they're rotting in hell with a tie still cinched around their throat.

I shrugged the shirt off and tossed it onto the bed beside Zayd. He didn't say anything, just watched me the way he always did—quiet, steady, like he was studying something important. From one of the boxes I'd half-unpacked, I pulled out a black t-shirt, simple, and tugged it over my head. Cotton. Soft. Real.

"Even back then, we were already drifting," I went on, my voice catching rough in my throat. "And when I left... that drift became something else. He was furious. Rightfully so. But this place was killing me. Staying here, under Cesare's roof, under his thumb—" I let out a humorless laugh. "It was unbearable."

I fell back onto the mattress, letting it take me. For a moment, I thought about never getting up. Zayd's fingers slipped into my hair, slow and unhurried, the kind of touch that told me he wasn't going anywhere. His silence was the kind I liked—the kind that listened.

"Am I talking too much?" I asked, chuckling, though it came out hollow.

"No," he murmured, and his voice was warm, patient. "I like listening to you."

He always had. Even centuries ago, when I was Philetos, running my mouth about everything and nothing—he was steady, anchoring me when I couldn't anchor myself.

I stared at the ceiling, tracing the cracks spidering through the plaster. Were they new, or had they been there my whole life, and I'd just never noticed? "Do you think he hates me?"

Zayd's fingers stilled for a moment, just the briefest pause, before they resumed their slow, deliberate strokes. "I don't think he hates you." His voice was thoughtful, like he was picking his words carefully. "I think he feels... lost. Unseen. He's here, waiting for something, but nothing's come. And when you left, Silas, it made that feeling worse."

"And now that I'm back, it's like salt in the wound. I've got a purpose handed to me on a silver platter, and he's still stuck, waiting for something that'll never come." I sighed, bitter laughter bubbling up. "So, yeah, he hates me."

"He's a grown man. It's not anyone's job to give him purpose. That has to come from him."

I sighed again, heavier this time, rolling onto my side to face him. Zayd, always so composed, so still. I pulled him down to me, pressing my lips to his. His mouth curled into a faint smile against mine.

"Are you stalling?" he asked, the amusement in his voice soft but unmistakable.

"Maybe." The word was a chuckle, but it died quickly.

We were supposed to meet August at one of those sleek, glass-walled restaurants downtown. The kind of place that charged a fortune for scraps of food and called it art. Everyone knew it was just another laundering front, appearances polished until they gleamed. People went because they wanted to believe in the illusion. Just like everything else in this life.

When we stepped inside, the place was empty. No guests, no staff. Just the faint hum of background music, the kind that was meant to fade into the atmosphere, leaving nothing but the pristine, cold design. Polished smooth floors, black leather chairs, and steel fixtures that gleamed under the dim lights. Every inch of it screamed wealth, success. Power.

"Hey." August's voice snapped me out of it. He was leaning against the bar, arms crossed, watching us.

"You cleared it out just for us?" I asked, my words carrying the faintest laugh, though I didn't feel it.

He shrugged, casual in movement, sharp in the eyes. "Can't exactly talk family business with a crowd."

I drifted toward the bar, my fingertips brushing the wood—sleek, polished, soulless. It was beautiful in the way a coffin is beautiful: perfect, untouched, sterile. Not like the Grove & Grain. My bar—well, Ivy's now—was worn down at the edges, scarred with fingerprints and spilled drinks, carrying warmth in its bones. This place? This was a showroom, not a heartbeat.

"I thought it might be fun to have you make us something," August said, sitting down at one of the stools, his gaze watching me closely. "Show me what was so damn special about bartending that you left us for it."

There it was. The passive-aggressiveness. I knew it was coming, but it still stung. It was going to take more than a few drinks to fix the mess between us.

"If you didn't want to pay for a bartender, you could've just said so," I said lightly, ducking behind the counter. Zayd sat beside him, quiet, letting the two of us circle our mess without interference.

August's fingers traced the edge of the wood, his gaze drifting somewhere far away. "How come you never invited me to your place? The bar."

I froze for half a breath, then pulled down a few glasses, buying time. "I wanted to keep that life separate. I didn't want... this"—I gestured vaguely around us, the steel, the money, the legacy that had its claws in both of us—"to bleed into it."

"So, you didn't want me there."

"That's not what I said."

"But it's what you meant."

I sighed inwardly, the kind that starts in your bones and coils in your chest, knowing how awkward this had to be for Zayd—sitting here, caught between two Vassallo men circling each other like dogs with too much history.

"If you'd asked to come," I said, my voice even but strained, "if you'd wanted to be there with me—I would've given you the address in a heartbeat. You know that."

I poured the drinks in silence. The sound of liquor meeting glass was louder than it should've been, a sharp punctuation in the heavy air. The scent rose up, rich and biting, the cool weight of the glass grounding me. I took a swallow. It burned on the way down, but I welcomed it—the warmth unfurling through me like an old friend. Something solid to hold on to.

August didn't touch his glass. Just stared at it, waiting. He always did that—waited, patient as a knife resting on a table. I knew what he wanted. The real answer. The one I hadn't said out loud yet.

"There was an emptiness here," I finally said, setting my drink down, leaning forward until the bar's cold surface kissed my forearms. "Not because of you. Not because of our mother. It was something else. Something neither of you could fill."

My words slowed, heavy, like dragging stones out of water. "My whole life was laid out for me. From the start. I was meant to step into power, build the family name, carry the weight. And for a while, I thought I could. I thought maybe I wanted it. I liked the deals, the control... even the violence." My throat caught, just for a second. Enough for me to hear it. "Then I realized—I was becoming him. I was becoming Cesare."

The silence pressed close around me. "And I couldn't let that happen. I wasn't going to be the man I despised. I wasn't going to carry that cycle forward, hand it down like a curse. So I left. I went looking for something that was mine. Something that was *me*."

My gaze met his.

"And yet here you are," he said, his voice smooth as the liquor untouched in his hand. "Walking back onto the path Cesare carved for you. Claiming it again, without ever having to work for it."

The words landed sharp, surgical. I felt the sting settle beneath my ribs, heat rising to meet it. He wouldn't understand. How could he? Cesare wasn't the only one who'd carved my fate. The Theion had their hands in it too, weaving threads Zayd swore I couldn't cut, no matter how hard I tried. My death was already out there, waiting for me like an old debt. The Callaghans were just the ones holding the knife this time.

But the truth? Maybe Legare's throne offered better protection than any quiet bar ever could. Maybe this time, power meant survival.

But that wasn't something August would hear. Not tonight.

"So who are you, Silas?" August asked, his voice calm in that way that wasn't really calm at all. Too measured. His eyes were dark, full of something I couldn't name—resentment, maybe, or just the echo of it. "What did this great self-discovered path lead you to? Because from where I'm standing, it looks like you crawled back the second it got easier—once you didn't have to deal with Father."

"I don't know." The words scraped out of me, heavier than I meant them to be. My chest tightened, guilt curling like smoke inside me. "Do you even know who *you* are?"

He shrugged, lazy, like this whole thing barely grazed him anymore. "Does it matter? I'm in the same boat as you. My path was laid out too. The difference is, I had to prove I earned it. My place could've been ripped out from under me the moment Father was displeased."

That much was true. August was groomed for Sottocapo, the seat just under mine. But until he and I figured out how to stop circling each other like this, Arnaldo wore that title. And if August kept bristling, if he couldn't let go of whatever it was he held against me, Arnaldo would keep it.

"Why do I feel like you're pissed that I'm back?" I asked before I could bite the words down, the blunt edge of my frustration cutting through.

"I'm sorry you feel that way." His tone was smooth, polite, but there wasn't a shred of apology in it. Just the mask he'd gotten too good at wearing. "I'm not pissed you're back."

Bullshit. The lie sat plain between us, but I was too tired to rip it apart. The silence stretched thin, taut, like a thread that could snap at any second.

"Are you going back to college?" I asked, groping for something lighter, something to fill the space between us.

He laughed, dry and humorless. "Seems a little ironic, doesn't it? Going to school to save lives when taking them has become so... normal."

I chuckled despite myself, the sound rough and hollow.

And then he shifted, his eyes flicking to Zayd with a sharpness that unsettled me. "Where are my manners?" August's smile was faint, more a mask than anything genuine. "I looked into you. It's only natural, considering someone new has entered this space. How exactly does someone from a philanthropic consulting firm end up dating a bartender?" His head tilted, eyes narrowing as he studied Zayd.

Zayd answered calmly, his voice a thread of warmth that smoothed over the tension. He spun our story with a grace I hadn't expected, his words soft but sure. It sounded different coming from him—more romantic, more deliberate. I hadn't realized how well Zayd could weave words together, how his centuries of blending in with mortals had made him so adept at storytelling. At lying.

The next hour slipped by in small talk, a hollow kind of ease. We skimmed across the surface of things we should've broken into, both of us experts at avoidance when it served us best.

By the time we stepped out, the night air sank cold into my skin, bracing, merciless. I was ready for the usual parting, something curt, maybe a glance that said nothing and too much all at once. But August surprised me—pulled me into a hug so sudden it stiffened my spine. His breath ghosted close to my ear, his words soft but deliberate.

"I always knew where you were," he murmured. "I did come for you. I sent two men to bring you back. I just expected they'd return you... without a pulse."

My jaw locked, muscles straining as my pulse quickened, a hot rush against the cold bite of his words. They clung to me, heavier than the air, colder than anything I'd prepared myself to hear.

"If you want something done right," August whispered, pulling back just enough for me to see the twisted curve of his smile, "you do it yourself."

Chapter Eighteen

Zayd

"What—" Silas' words fell away as the crack of the gunshot tore through the parking lot, shattering the fragile stillness of the night.

I didn't register the sound at first, didn't register the blood blooming like some cursed flower against his shirt, or the way his body recoiled from the force. My mind, sluggish, grappled with the reality before me, and I found myself whispering his name, a plea more than a call. "Silas..."

It was as though the world had grown heavier in that instant, like time had splintered, dragged itself out into an agonizing crawl. And yet, my body moved forward, as if pulled by some invisible string, propelling me toward him. Toward Silas, who stepped back from August, his hand pressed against his chest—just below where his heart is. Slow, deliberate, as though he didn't quite believe it himself. As though he, too, couldn't understand what was happening.

By the time I reached him, his legs were faltering, and I caught him just as his knees gave way.

"Silas," I whispered again, my voice cracking, barely more than a breath. I lowered us both to the ground, his weight cradled against me, but his eyes—they weren't on me. They stayed on his brother.

Augustus stood there, frozen, his hand still gripping the gun as though he had forgotten how to release it. The tip of it gleamed in the dim light, slick with Silas' blood. There was no triumph in his face, no remorse—just emptiness. A hollow man staring into the abyss he had created.

"I—" Augustus tried to speak, but Eryx was already there, materializing from the shadows like a storm, his hand wrapping around the gun, wrenching it away. The sound of metal meeting bone as he struck him echoed through the space. And then, silence, as Augustus' body hit the ground with a dull thud.

But I couldn't focus on him.

My hands moved of their own accord, pressing down over Silas' wound, though the blood spilled through my fingers faster than I could contain it. It felt like trying to hold back the tide.

I had seen this before. I had lived this before. The life seeping away, just as it had all those centuries ago. Philetos. My beautiful Philetos. I had failed him then, and now...

I couldn't fail again.

"*Me ti thélisi ton Theíon, eímai to ergaleío tous, to óplo tous...*" The words, ancient and sacred, slipped from my lips unbidden, a prayer, a demand for my sealed off power to seep through just this once. "*I aspída tous, to theío réei mésa apó ména, kai tóra se séna.*"

Nothing. No response. His blood still flowed, hot and thick, over my hands, painting the ground beneath us.

I tilted my head back, staring up at the sky as though the gods themselves might peer down and take pity, as though they would hear me, for once, and grant me this one, desperate plea.

"Zayd..." Eryx's voice broke through the haze, but I couldn't look at him. I knew what he would say. He wanted me to stop, to accept it. To let Silas go, to let fate have its way with him.

But I couldn't.

I pressed harder, my hands slick with his blood, teeth gritting as I repeated the words, louder now, more insistent. "*Me ti thélisi ton Theíon, eímai to ergaleío tous...*"

Please. I couldn't do this again. Not again. Not him. Not Silas.

"Zayd." Silas' voice was softer now, directed towards me, I could feel his breath on my skin. His hand, slick with blood, rose to clasp mine, gently prying my fingers away from the wound. "Stop."

I couldn't meet his gaze. I couldn't look at him. Not now.

His thumb brushed against my cheek, smearing blood in its wake. He turned my face toward him, his eyes—so dark, so tired—met mine. "No matter what, we will still find each other," he promised, his voice so quiet I had to strain to hear it. "Just be here with me, in this moment, okay?"

I swallowed hard, my throat tight as I nodded, though my heart warred with every beat, desperate to fight, to claw him back from the edge. But I could only hold him as he rested his head against my cheek, his breathing growing shallow.

"You're pouting again," he whispered, the faintest smile touching his lips.

"Can you blame me?" I said, a weak laugh escaping despite the weight crushing my chest.

Mortals could die of a broken heart, and yet I was expected to endure this. To watch him slip away.

"It's not your fault," he murmured, his words echoing Philetos' from so long ago, as though he didn't want to leave me with that burden I have been carrying any longer. As if he didn't want the guilt to continue to devour me. But I will continue to carry it. I always will.

"It's not..." His head slumped slowly to lower against my chest, and I felt his heartbeat falter, a weak flutter under my fingers.

"Silas..." My voice broke. "Philetos..."

I tightened my grip around him, calling the mists of Khaos to envelop us. Our forms flickered between worlds—the mortal realm and Khaos, the divine realm pulling at me, trying to take me there. But my form resisted, straining to hold onto Silas, to pull him with me. This was the domain of the divine, where time slowed and bent. Where mortals were only welcomed if they were dead, so they could pass through the mists to reach Erebos.

What do I have left to lose? What more can they take from me?

I fought against the mists, my body burning, torn between realms, unsure where I belonged as I clung desperately to a mortal soul.

I couldn't let go. I wouldn't let go.

I pushed, calling the Khaos with all the divinity that remained in me.

Silence finally engulfed us. The world, the very air, was muted, enshrouded in the thick mist.

"Zayd, what are you doing?" Eryx's voice pierced through the quiet. He stepped closer, crouching in front of me, and instinctively, I pulled Silas tighter against me.

I was stalling—buying time. Time moved differently here, and I wasn't ready to let him go. I couldn't. I couldn't.

"Zayd, he's already dead." Eryx's voice was gentle, as if afraid his words would shatter me.

"No, he's not." My voice was trembling, the tears hot against my cheeks. I could still feel it—the faint thrum of life. "I felt it, the pulse. He's not dead."

"You have to bring him back so his soul can leave his body. It needs to go to the mists on its own."

"He's not dead!" I shouted, glaring at him through the tears, my voice breaking under the weight of the truth I refused to accept.

"Zayd..." His voice wavered, a crack in his usual coolness. "Look at him."

I couldn't.

"Look at him!"

Slowly, I forced my eyes down to Silas' face, but there was no light behind those eyes. Just emptiness. Stillness.

The gods had taken him. They had taken Philetos from me again.

I pressed my lips to his hair, a broken plea falling from my mouth. "Take me with you. Please... I am not for a life without you."

Moments of silence passed as my pleas filled the air of Khaos before finally Eryx rose, stepping back a few paces, his gaze lifting through the swirling mists, up toward the heavens, toward Aither. "Take me," he whispered, though the words weren't meant for me.

He was speaking to the Theion.

Chapter Nineteen

Eryx

"Take me," I breathed, my voice low, fragile, like it might break with the weight of the words. My gaze flickered up, searching the mists above. Though I could not see them, I knew they watched from beyond the veil. "You want balance? A Daimon's soul is worth more than a mortal's."

Zayd's sobs quieted, his brow furrowing as his tear-streaked face lifted toward me. "What are you doing?"

"They don't care about mortals or Daimons." I spoke to the air, not to him. There was a slight tremble in my voice I couldn't mask, but I stood, more certain than ever. "They only care about balance."

The weight of Khaos pressed in, the mist swirling in endless coils, alive and watching. It was always watching. *They* were always watching. Their silence was deafening, the space between heartbeats stretched thin as if all of creation waited for the choice I was about to make.

"Take me!" I shouted into the void, louder this time, more demanding. I felt the mists recoil and twist, and for a moment, I wondered if they heard me at all.

I don't know what drove me that day millenniums ago. Maybe it was curiosity, that same gnawing curiosity that had always festered within me. Always building, always hungering. That day, I had ventured closer than I should have, desperate to see something—anything—that broke the monotony of eternity. I had witnessed the first forsaken, and it wasn't horror or violence that had struck me. No, it was something else. Something unexpected.

A smile.

Not directed at me, of course. It never had been. A smile directed towards a memory that clouded the mind. But it didn't matter. It was the most beautiful thing I had ever seen, a flash of something pure. Before that moment, I don't think I even knew what beauty was.

I couldn't help myself. I took that forsaken Eudaimon, Zayd, off the spike that day, just to see it again. To selfishly have that glimpse of beauty with me at all times.

And that became my goal. My obsession. To make him smile. I didn't care who it was truly for—whether it was for me, or Philetos, or some distant memory. I just needed to see it.

I think the more time we spent together, the more I became more like the Eudai. Perhaps that was why it has always been that way, the Daimons divided. Why we were made to believe that the Kakodaimons and Eudaimons were opposing forces. A balance was needed. Light and shadow, joy and sorrow—one could not exist without the other. But the Theions couldn't allow an imbalance, and maybe... it wasn't just Zayd that had tipped the scales too far.

Zayd's voice pulled me from my thoughts, his eyes red and pained, the way they always were when he watched Philetos die—but now directed to me. "Eryx, stop this!"

The Theions didn't need to say a word. They never did. But I felt it—the shift, the slow unraveling of my form, like I was being pulled apart, thread by thread. My edges frayed, my shape losing definition as if I were passing through something solid, becoming mist myself.

"I'd rather cease to exist, than to watch you become a shell of what you once were," I said softly. My throat felt tight, my chest hollow, but something was lightening. "You wouldn't truly be here. A world without you in it is dull. I refuse to live in that."

His voice was raw with grief. "Eryx, this isn't your punishment to bear."

But it wasn't about punishment anymore. It hadn't been for a long time. "Zayd, think of it as a favor." I forced a smile, though I wasn't sure if it even showed on my fading form. "Pay me back by smiling. Smile as much as you can... I'll be watching you, my little Eudai. So don't let me down."

Would I even be able to see that smile again? This was uncharted territory—for me, for the Theions, for all of us.

"Promise me," I whispered. My vision blurred, a wetness trailing down my cheeks. Was this sadness? Is this what it felt like to grieve? And yet... the heaviness that had clung to me for so long was lifting.

"Zayd, promise me..." My voice was growing weaker, fainter, dissolving like smoke in the air.

"I promise," he choked out, his words barely a breath.

I tried to laugh, but no sound came. It was all fading too quickly now. I wished I had more time. More time to watch, more time to see—

And then... *there it is.*

Despite everything, I saw it. Zayd's lips twitched, the corners lifting ever so slightly. It wasn't forced, wasn't something he did out of pity or pain. It was real, a true smile breaking through the sorrow.

Three simple words passed his lips, though I couldn't hear them. I couldn't hear anything anymore. But I swear, in that moment, I felt warmth spread through my chest.

Was this... love?

I didn't know, not truly. But as the mist swallowed me whole, that smile stayed with me. And for the first time in my endless existence, I felt like I had done something right.

Chapter Twenty

Zayd

The sterile hum of fluorescent lights buzzed faintly overhead, as the cold air of the hospital room settled into my bones. The smell—sharp, metallic, tainted with antiseptic—laced with something more. Desperation, death, and despair. Hospitals, no matter the century, always carried that same cruel scent. A place where lives frayed at the edges, unraveling like the loose ends of a threadbare tapestry. Yet this time, amid the cruelness, there was a kind of solace. Silas was here, and breathing.

I leaned closer, fingers brushing away the unruly strands of golden blond that clung stubbornly to his brow. His face was still too pale, though a faint flush of color had begun to seep back into his skin. Each breath he took, shallow but steady, was a fragile victory against the odds. Silas clung to life with a will as fierce as any I had ever known but if it were not for the Theion, *no*, Eryx, we wouldn't be in this place.

The gunshot wound was fired too close, too sudden, it had torn through him, causing him to lose too much blood at such a rapid pace. He had died, briefly. His heart had faltered, stilled when we returned to the mortal realm. But the doctors... they had pulled him back, stitched together the life that had slipped from his grasp.

The door creaked open, breaking the silence. The soft tap of heels against the tile echoed in the room, and Alessia entered with her usual softness. She carried with her that same sense of quiet control, a veneer of calm over what I knew must have been a roiling storm beneath. "The doctors say it's hard to know when he'll wake," she said, her voice laced with fragile hope. "But his body is strong. The surgery went as well as it could."

She moved to his side, brushing her lips to his forehead with the tenderness only a mother could possess. "I know none of this is what you asked for," she said, glancing at me as though I were just another outsider swept into the chaos of her son's life. She had no idea how deeply my existence was entwined with his.

"I hope you'll keep how this happened between us. For Silas' sake," she continued, her fingers tracing the line of his arm as though she could protect him with a touch. "As for Augustus... it's been handled. We saw how he was unraveling, but I should have stepped in sooner."

I met her eyes briefly, offering a weak attempt at reassurance. "I don't think anyone could have foreseen this," I replied, though even as I spoke, a knot twisted in my gut. I had seen it. In glimpses, in flickers—signs that Augustus' resentment was festering, swelling into something darker. But not this. Not a betrayal this violent, not with his own hand.

Perhaps if I had warned Silas, told him of how Augustus was working with the Callaghans. Of what he had done to me—how he had taken me, blindfolded and bound, and was going to use me as bait—then maybe Silas would have been prepared. Maybe he would have seen the madness coming. But I had hoped sparing Augustus' life that day had been enough to appease his fractured mind. I had been wrong.

"He's getting help," Alessia continued, her voice quiet but firm, as though willing it to be true. "With some of the best in the country. Psychologists, psychiatrists. But discretion is important, especially if you plan to be part of our family. If you plan to be with Silas."

There was a weight to her words, an unspoken warning hidden beneath the soft cadence of her voice. She was beautiful, yes, but there was a steel beneath her elegance. A quiet, unyielding power that both demanded respect and inspired fear.

"I love your son," I said, the words slipping from me so easily. My hand found Silas', cold but still warm enough to reassure me. I lifted it to my lips, pressing a kiss to the back of his hand. "I want to marry him. To spend my life with him."

Alessia's gaze softened, though I could feel the assessment behind it. "You and him don't need my permission if you wish to marry," she said after a moment, "but you do have my blessing. And Legare's."

Her words had brought relief, but also anticipation, my heart raced, each beat thudding heavily in my chest. What could I say in return? How could I express the depth of what Silas meant to me, how my existence had been shaped by the centuries I had spent without him, and with him.

"Thank you," was all I managed, though it felt insufficient.

"Take care of him," she said softly, almost a plea. "He has a big heart. It's what makes him who he is."

Yes, I thought. That was the truth of Philetos—the core of him that transcended lifetimes, that pulled me back to him again and again. His capacity to love, to care and feel so deeply, was unlike anything I had ever known. It was what drew me to him, that beautiful, untarnished light within him. It was woven into everything he did, from his art to his family, to the way he looked at me like I was the only thing in the world that mattered. Even in this life, surrounded by shadows, that light never dimmed.

A weariness had settled over me, heavier than anything I had known in all my years, clinging to my bones, dragging me down into the hard-backed chair as though the weight of centuries had finally caught up. The sterile tang of antiseptic hung in the air, sharp and intrusive, yet not even that could anchor me fully in the present. The steady, rhythmic beeping of the heart monitor, a monotonous pulse of life, became the only sound I could latch onto.

I let myself drift, sinking into a half-wakeful slumber where the lines between consciousness and the unyielding void of sleep blurred, and soon, the slumber found me.

When I opened my eyes, it was not to the hospital's harsh lights but to the familiar embrace of the Khaos, its mist swirling around me, beckoning me back to its endless, unknowable depths. And with it, Malaika. She moved toward me like a whisper, her form soft and ethereal, as though she were a dream herself, the gentle flutter of her snowy wings stirring the air between us.

"This is the last time you will feel the mists, Zayd. Until Erebos comes for you," she said, her voice carrying the weight of inevitability.

I shook my head, the dregs of sleep still clinging to my thoughts. "I don't understand." My words felt hollow, a feeble protest against the truth that had begun to unfurl within me, slow and inexorable.

Her gaze softened, a sorrow there that mirrored my own, though I knew she would never allow it to touch her words. "You feel it, don't you, brother?" she asked, her tone gentle yet insistent. "Mortality... slipping in."

"Mortality..." I echoed, the word foreign on my tongue, as though it did not belong to me. It felt like an absurdity—me, becoming mortal, shackled to the frailty of flesh, the relentless march of time.

Malaika clicked her tongue softly, as if chastising a child who should know better. "Time and time again, you defy the Theion. And now, you are surprised. You brought a mortal into Khaos, Zayd. You briefly shattered the boundary between our worlds." Her wings shifted slightly, a ripple of tension, but her voice remained steady. "And for that, you are to be punished. They've stripped your wings, and now... your divine grace. You are no longer Daimon."

Her words settled over me like the weight of a tombstone. Mortal. The word was cold, final, without room for debate or reason. The idea of it gnawed at the edges of my mind. I had known punishment, yes. I had endured the loss of my wings, the exile from the celestial heights. But this... this was an end I had not anticipated.

Malaika's voice softened as she continued, "Once I return you to the mortal realm, you will be human, Zayd. Fully. There will be no reincarnation for you or Silas. You will live, and you will die, as mortals do." She hesitated, a rare flicker of compassion passing over her features. "Live this life with him. Do not let Eryx's sacrifice be in vain."

Her gaze shifted, looking through the muted mists to Silas before settling back on me. "Though you are not immortal, the tales of you will be. First Daimon to defy the Theion. First Daimon to love," Malaika mused, watching me with an intensity. "And now, you are the first to fall to mortality. It seems you are the beginning of the firsts, Zayd. "

I met her gaze, unflinching, though inside, the knowledge twisted something deep within me. "Perhaps I am a cautionary tale," I murmured, my voice tight, controlled, though I could feel the edges of my composure fraying.

Her smile was faint, sad. "No, Zayd. You are something far more than that. Eryx, will not be forgotten either. He had firsts for us too. He was the first Daimon to return to the cycle. From mortal soul in Erebos to Daimon, and then to Erebos once more" She paused, her eyes searching mine, seeking some acknowledgment of the truth she was about to reveal. "First Daimon to love another Daimon."

The words struck with the force of a revelation, though they should not have. I had always known, hadn't I? Somewhere deep beneath the surface of all my denial, the truth had always been there, a quiet, unspoken thing.

"Oh, Zayd, surely you cannot be so unaware? Were you so consumed by your love for man that you failed to see what was right before your eyes?"

I swallowed hard, the knowledge heavy in my chest. Had Eryx known he loved me? It was not something that came naturally to Kakodaimons, even less so compared to Eudaimons. Yet, there had always been something between us—a quiet, unspoken bond that tethered us through the centuries, stronger than anything else. He had been my constant, my anchor through these endless millennia.

And I for him. Perhaps we had loved each other all along, but neither of us ever knew to speak it—not until the very end, when words finally failed us, and we let our other ways speak what our hearts had known all along.

"Stay with me," I had spoke to him, my voice barely holding. It was the last thing I said to him, words I had spoken before—words he had always answered, without hesitation, until that final moment.

"The mortals say it is possible to have more than one soul mate, more than one love." Malaika said lightly, though her gaze was knowing, as though she took some small pleasure in watching me struggle with the enormity of what I had missed. "A notion to think about. Humans, with their endless romanticizing of everything."

Her laughter was soft, musical, a sound that somehow seemed distant now, as though it belonged to a different world. And perhaps it did.

"Enjoy this life, Zayd. Experience what we cannot." And with that, the mists of Khaos began to pull away, leaving me with nothing but the weight of mortality pressing in.

Chapter Twenty-One

Silas

My eyelids felt like stone, lifting slow, reluctant, as though they hadn't bothered in days. Maybe they hadn't. The world returned in fragments—a wash of blurred light bleeding through a window, the low hum of machines, the faint shift of fabric against a chair. And then, there he was.

Zayd.

He sat beside me, still as a statue, his gaze fixed somewhere past the room, past me. Sunlight cut across him in soft gold, threading through his hair, outlining him like something not quite of this world. Untouchable. Ethereal. Like if I blinked too long, he'd dissolve back into the dream I must've crawled out of.

My throat burned, the words scraping out of me broken, but I forced them anyway. "Careful," I rasped, my lips quirking with effort, "thinking that hard'll give you a headache."

It wasn't much, but it was mine—a thin, cracked attempt at humor.

His head snapped toward me, eyes wide, and just like that he wasn't distant anymore. He was alive, his composure splintering in an instant. "Silas," he whispered, my name spilling from him like it hurt to say, his lips trembling with the weight of it. For all the centuries he'd worn his masks, I was the one who made them slip. And gods, it undid me every time.

"If you're gonna stare at me like that, you might as well hug me," I croaked, pushing the words out with more need than charm.

He was on me before I could breathe another syllable, arms folding around me—gentle, careful, like I was glass. His weight pressed to my chest, and pain flickered sharp under my ribs, but I bit it down. He moved to pull away, of course he did, but I caught him, tightening my hold, grounding myself in him.

"Stay," I muttered, low, rough, my desperation bleeding through despite myself.

His breath brushed against my neck, warm, hesitant. "I don't want to hurt you."

"Not hugging me hurts me," I murmured back, half-laugh, half-plea, and entirely true.

That got him—the faintest smile breaking through the sorrow in his face. It sat there, fragile, like he wasn't sure he was allowed to feel it.

He pulled back just enough to find my eyes, his gaze searching, steady. "Do you remember what happened?"

I frowned, trying to claw something out of the fog that clung to my skull. "I'll be real with you... not much." My mouth twisted into a weak, humorless laugh. "I think—I think I died?" The sound cracked in my throat, hollow, like even my own voice didn't buy it. But some part of me still swore I'd crossed a line I wasn't meant to come back from.

"You did," he said, quiet, certain. No comfort in it, no softening. Just the truth, bare and cruel.

I blinked at him, forcing myself to breathe through the sharp press of that word. "But I'm not dead now. So—how? I thought I was supposed to die."

Something shifted in his eyes then, something deep, ancient, a sorrow so quiet it was louder than anything he could've said. And then the words came.

He told me about Eryx. About Malaika. About August. Things he had never said before, pieces he'd carried like knives in his chest, pulling them out now one by one, laying them bloody between us. Each word drew the line clearer between life and death, between the mortals we pretended to be and the divine bastards—the Theion—whose games were beyond my reach, beyond even the fragments I remembered of when they walked freely among us. They were always distant, always untouchable.

But when he shifted, when his voice turned toward his own mortality, something inside me twisted sharp. My heart sank like a stone through dark water.

"What if I can't protect you?" The words slipped loose before I could stop them. My mind went back to before all this, before Philetos' memories came crashing in—back when all I wanted was to keep him away from this life. To keep him clean of it, untouched by the blood, by the weight, by the constant shadow of threat. I'd wanted peace for us. A world where we didn't have to look over our shoulders.

His gaze caught mine, steady, unflinching. "I think you keep forgetting—I'm not fragile," he said, his tone calm, carved in certainty. "I can keep myself safe. I can handle whatever comes. If you want to leave Legare, I'll leave with you. If you want to stay, I'll stand beside you. As long as we're together, we'll face it all. *Together*."

And gods help me—I believed him. The way he said it made me believe. For just a heartbeat, it felt possible—that we could take on the world and live. That maybe, if I held onto him tightly enough, together really was enough.

The nurse slapped a visitor's badge against my chest like I was property, branded for entry. The tiles underfoot gleamed, polished to the kind of sterile perfection that made me itch. Too clean, too pristine—like no one had ever bled here, like no one had ever lost their mind screaming behind the walls. The paint was some muted, soothing shade I couldn't name. Calming, sure. If you were blind. To me it just screamed money.

Wellness Center. That's what they called it. As if a fancy name and a garden view made it anything more than a cage with better upholstery.

It had been months since they committed August. Months since I crawled back from the edge myself, stitched together in body if not in mind. My scars had healed, but the sound of that gunshot still cracked through me whenever the room went quiet. I told myself I didn't need to see him, didn't need to face him. Another lie. The question chewed at me too much. Why? Why pull the trigger on me—his own brother? Was it power? Was it Legare? Or was it something else I was too stupid—or too cowardly—to see?

The nurse led me down a hall that reeked of lavender and disinfectant, some sick cocktail of spa day and sterilization. It looked more like a resort than a psych hospital—high ceilings, manicured gardens outside, not a single scuff mark on the floor. If you ignored the locks, the cameras, the orderlies watching too closely, you might actually believe the illusion.

Finally, we stopped at his "room." Room was a generous term. It was bigger than my first apartment, with glass doors opening onto a private patio like they were rewarding him for losing his mind in style. Sunlight spilled in, warm, golden, like the universe had conspired to make the scene look peaceful.

But it didn't feel peaceful. It felt wrong.

August sat outside at a small table, his back to me, staring into the forest beyond. Still as stone. Like he belonged to that silence.

"Mr. Vassallo, you have a visitor," the nurse murmured, eyes fixed anywhere but mine. She didn't need to say it, but I could see it in the stiffness of her shoulders, the way she fidgeted with her clipboard—she knew. Knew what he'd done, or at least enough to guess that brothers didn't always mean safe.

Pericolo nella familiarità.

I stood there, stuck between the doorframe and my own pulse, trying to figure out what the hell you're supposed to say to someone who already killed you once. *Hi, how've you been? Sorry about the blood?*

I forced myself forward. The air in his room clung heavy, like it wanted to choke me before we even got started. This wasn't going to fix anything. I wasn't looking for some miracle confession to wipe the slate clean. I just needed the truth. Even if it cracked what was left of us straight down the middle.

August didn't move. Didn't even glance my way. Just sat there on the patio, his back straight, his hands folded neatly on the table, staring out into the trees like he'd finally made peace with the world. For a second, I almost didn't recognize him. He looked calm. Detached. That was worse. That he could sit in this manicured quiet while I still carried the chaos he'd left behind carved into my ribs.

"August." His name left my mouth raw, metallic, like blood.

Nothing. Not a twitch. Not a breath spared for me.

I took the chair across from him, the silence pressing down like a weight strapped to my chest. "Augustus." This time my voice cracked sharp, jagged. That finally got him. His gaze shifted—slow, deliberate—and the fake calm in his eyes slipped, replaced with the same quiet discontent I knew too well. A look that said *I was fine until you walked in.*

"You look well," he said, voice flat, too careful.

"You mean not dead." The words came out before I could dress them up.

"Yeah."

"Does that upset you?" I asked, my voice hardening, the edge of anger creeping in. He didn't answer, just looked down at the sleeve of his sweater, fingers absentmindedly playing with the fabric, like he had nothing more to offer me than silence.

"Why did you try to kill me?" I asked, leaning forward, elbows digging into my knees. My voice stayed steady somehow, though the knot in my chest pulled tighter.

He didn't hesitate this time. "I thought the answer was obvious. You were in my way." His eyes drifted back to the trees, as if they had more to offer than I did.

I swallowed hard, the words sitting heavy in the air between us. "Do you hate me?"

His jaw shifted, the pause deliberate, cruel in its slowness. And then: "The answer is more complex than you think. But to speak plainly... yes."

The hit landed clean, like a knife to the gut. I'd braced myself for it—prepared for the worst—but hearing it straight from his mouth was a different kind of wound. No blood this time, but the cut went deeper all the same.

I sat there staring at him, waiting for something, anything, that would explain what I'd done to deserve being his target. But there was nothing. Just silence, just trees, and the hollow truth between us.

"Why? What have I ever done to you?"

His eyes finally met mine. No fire there, no triumph. Just... emptiness. "Nothing."

The word landed harder than any bullet. Nothing. No hidden knife, no buried reason. Just hate for the sake of it, as if my existence alone was enough.

I stared at him, waiting for the punchline, for the mask to crack. But he wasn't lying. He wasn't hiding. It really was that simple. And that impossibly complicated.

"I don't understand," I muttered, the words catching in my throat, thick and bitter.

He shrugged, casual, like we were discussing the weather. "Sometimes people just hate. There isn't always a reason, Silas. Feelings don't need to be justified. They just are."

I dragged my palms down my face, a rough laugh breaking out of me despite the sting behind my eyes. "I still love you, you know." The laugh twisted sharp, hollow. "Guess you're right. Sometimes there isn't a reason. Because I shouldn't. Not after everything. But I do. I want the best for you anyway. How's that for stupid?"

The chair screeched against the tile as I stood, the sound slicing through the silence. This wasn't what I came here for. No answers, no clarity. Just another wound with no clean edges. Hate without a reason. Love without one either.

I shouldn't have come.

"Silas." His voice stopped me at the door, softer now, something that brushed faintly against the brother I used to know. I didn't turn. Didn't give him my face. But I waited, because he'd always get the last word.

"If it's worth anything..." His tone thinned, frayed, and almost—almost—sounded like honesty. "I want you to know that I'm finally happy."

The words hung there, fragile and absurd, like glass in my hands. For a second, I almost believed him.

Then I walked out, leaving him to his happiness.

Chapter Twenty-Two

Zayd

My fingers moved carefully, smoothing over the silk of his tie, adjusting it with precision. Each loop, each tug, was deliberate, as though the very act of tying this knot would bind us closer together. "You know," I said softly, "most couples don't see each other before the altar."

"True," he agreed, his voice warm, a soft chuckle in the air between us. "But what's more fun and romantic than walking down the aisle with the love of your life? Instead of one of us waiting, we take the next steps as one."

I paused, my hands stilling on the fabric. "A journey taken together," I mused, almost to myself. "Destinations the same." My voice grew quieter, more fragile. "That is romantic, yes."

But even as I spoke, the air in the room felt heavy with something unspoken, something fragile and elusive. Too good to be true. The music beyond the walls—the delicate strains of the orchestra as it played for our guests—felt distant, like a memory rather than something happening now. I had dreamed of this moment, seen it in fragments over centuries, imagined it in all the ways one could imagine happiness, but always, always, it turned to smoke in my hands. Theion's will lingered in the back of my mind like a shadow, a reminder that joy could be fleeting.

His hand came to rest against my cheek, pulling me from my thoughts with the warmth of his touch. His gaze, steady and unwavering, met mine. "I think my tie is fine now, Zayd," he said with an amused smile. "You've been messing with it for five minutes now."

"Sorry," I murmured, the apology slipping from my lips. "I just..." But the words faltered and died on my tongue.

"Don't worry so much." His voice was soft, yet firm, grounding me. "Think about the here and now. Be with me in this moment. Being human means living in the present. If you keep worrying about the 'what ifs,' you'll miss what's right in front of you." He smiled, a soft and tenderness in his eyes.

"I don't want to miss a single moment with you," I breathed, the words coming from a deep place that only him and I could truly understand.

"Good." His smile widened, and he leaned in, closing the space between us for a kiss. But I raised a hand, pressing my fingers gently against his lips.

"Wait for the altar,"

He sighed, a playful, exaggerated sound. "Alright, alright." But he gripped my wrist before I could pull away, pressing a kiss against my palm. "That should hold me over until then," he muttered, his voice muffled against my skin, his eyes twinkling with mischief.

Our hands intertwined, the warmth of his fingers lacing through mine, and together we began our slow walk toward the doors of the temple nave, the grand wooden carvings that marked the beginning of a new chapter. I felt the shift in the air, the quiet hum of anticipation as the music from the quartet swelled. This was real. This was happening. And yet, it felt like something else, something out of time and space, something that existed only between us.

The melody shifted, flowing effortlessly into another tune—the one I had chosen for our walk down the aisle. The first chords swelled softly, spilling through the door like a whispered promise.

I glanced at Silas, and he was already looking at me, his brow furrowed in recognition, the softest smile pulling at his lips. It was his ballad, Philetos', the one he had composed so long ago. "How did you find it?" he asked, his voice thick with nostalgia. "I can't believe you still remembered."

"How could I forget?" I replied, my voice barely above a whisper. "It was the song you sang on the steps of the Parthenon when we first met." I remembered that day with a clarity that hurt—how I had watched him, Philetos then, his voice carrying through the air like the gods had placed each note in his throat. I had been sent to witness him, to help him become the poet he was destined to be, his songs to be passed down through the ages. But even the Theion had not prepared me for the power of him, for the way his voice, his very soul, had drawn me in like a tide.

He hummed along with the melody, the sound sending a shiver down my spine. "Did you know," he said softly, "the ending was inspired by you? I didn't know how to finish it until I saw you."

My heart caught in my throat as he continued, his eyes distant, remembering. "I didn't know beauty until I saw you," he confessed, his voice almost reverent. "And then I knew exactly how to end it."

I couldn't stop the smile that spread across my lips, nor the overwhelming urge to close the distance between us. I leaned in, pressing my lips to his, and for a moment, everything else ceased to exist—the temple, the music, the fear that lingered at the edges of my mind. There was only him, and the way his lips curved against mine in a smile.

"What happened to waiting for the altar?" he teased, his arms pulling me closer, his breath mingling with mine.

"Are you complaining?"

"Never," he whispered, pressing his lips to mine once more.

"*Caro*," Alessia's voice broke through, her tone gentle but firm, a reminder of the world beyond us. "You're supposed to wait for the altar."

"I tried to tell Zayd that," Silas said with a grin, stepping back reluctantly, "but he insisted."

Alessia looped her arms through mine and his, pulling us apart, her smile warm and knowing. "The song has already begun," she said. "Let's go."

And as we moved toward the doors, I glanced at him once more, at the warmth in his eyes, the promise of everything we would face together.

The inner sanctum of the temple was a place where time itself seemed to hang in suspension, caught between the marble columns and the faint echo of footsteps against the granite floors. The scent of incense, thick and sweet, curled through the air, mingling with the perfume of flowers—roses, lilies, and anemones. Though the gods were nameless now, traditions still continued and offerings were made in the name of marriage and love.

My gaze drifted above us as we walked. Painted across the high, vaulted ceilings, were scenes of forgotten myths adorned the stone in vivid, fading colors. The figures of gods and mortals intertwined, their stories mingling like smoke and memory, their essence clinging to the walls like whispers in the wind.

As we made our way down the aisle, we were met with the familiar faces of the Legare families and the rest of the Vassallo bloodline, their expressions soft with warmth, as they turned to greet us. These were Silas' people, his blood, his family—but soon, they would be mine too, in the way that such things are shared, woven together by vows and time. I could feel their eyes on us, not with judgment, but with quiet acceptance, though I knew well enough that this was not the day Cesare had envisioned for his son. Tradition had its grip on many, but Silas—Silas had always been more interested in carving his own path.

Alessia stood between us, her arm light through mine and his, a steady presence as we approached the altar. Yet as we neared, it was not the priestess or the altar that caught my attention, but a figure in the front pew. A face I knew all too well, though one I thought I would never see again. Malaika. Even in her modest, modern garb, she was unmistakable, her divine nature muted, but never fully hidden. Her dark hazel eyes rested on me—steady, unblinking, watching with something I couldn't place. Was it approval? A flicker of support? I had not expected her here, none of the Daimon for that matter.

"I didn't know you had a sister," Alessia murmured, leaning close as her breath brushed my ear. "But we made sure she was seated in the front, for you."

Sister. The word echoed in my mind, strange and hollow, but the kindness in her voice, warmth in Alessia's misunderstanding pulled a slight smile from me. I said nothing, only nodded.

Our gaze met once more and perhaps it was the way Malaika's gaze lingered, as though even in my forsaken state, I was still one of them, still her brother in spirit, if not in title. That gaze made part of my heart flutter in a way I had never felt.

My mind drifted, unbidden, to Eryx. He would be here, somewhere in the crowd if he were alive. He would not have missed this, not for the world, not even for the will of the Theion. I swallowed hard against the sudden swell of emotion in my chest, the way the memories tugged at the edges of my composure. The weight of a thousand unspoken things pressed against my ribs, but I bit them back, blinking away the moisture in my eyes.

As we reached the altar, Alessia left us, moving with quiet grace to join the others in the pews. The priestess awaited us, her robes a deep, rich red, with a golden palla draped over her head like a veil. Behind her, a towering statue of the divine feminine stood, arms outstretched, holding a brazier from which the fragrant incense billowed. It swirled like the breath of the Theion themselves, curling toward the vaulted ceiling.

Before the priestess, on a pedestal of its own, rested a golden bowl, gleaming in the soft light. Silas and I approached the pedestal in unison. The priestess' eyes on us were solemn but warm as her hands gracefully guided us through the ritual as she gestured toward the golden bowl. We each dipped our hands into the cool water, the weight of tradition pressing upon us—an offering of purity before the Theion, a cleansing that seemed more symbolic than necessary. Our fingertips brushed as we withdrew, a fleeting touch that sent a quiet current between us, unnoticed by all but felt deeply by me. It was as though, even in such a small gestures, we were binding ourselves together, piece by piece.

The priestess's voice rose, calling upon the Theion, invoking their ancient presence in words that felt as old as the stone beneath our feet. As she spoke on our behalf, petitioning for a marriage blessed with lasting devotion, I couldn't help but internally laugh. It was too ironic, really, asking for a blessing from the very Theion who had once cast me aside, condemned me to centuries of isolation and loss. The irony was not lost on Silas either; he gave me a sidelong glance, the corner of his mouth twitching into the faintest of smiles, a shared understanding passing between us. We were both well aware of the absurdity, and yet, we honored the tradition because there was something sacred in it, even for us. Perhaps especially for us.

When we joined hands, his brown eyes, so achingly like home, locked onto mine, and I could see the flicker of hesitation before he spoke. Silas, always so quick with words, now faltered as if the gravity of what he was about to say had caught up to him.

"I've always been shit with words, you know that," he began, his voice rough, unpolished in a way that made it all the more sincere, all the more Silas. "But I'm going to try, 'cause I want to get this right. Zayd, you walked into my life like a gift from the gods. You brought pieces of me together I didn't know were missing. You gave me a purpose without even meaning to."

He paused, and in the silence, I could hear the faint rustle of fabric, the distant murmur of the gathered family behind us. But in that moment, there was only him, only us.

"You've been a given for me. You see me—the good, the bad, the messed-up parts I don't show anyone—and you stay. You stay when I'm angry, when I'm scared, when I don't have the words for what's clawing at me inside. And that... that means more to me than I'll ever be able to say. I won't promise perfection. I'm not that guy. But I do promise this: I'll stand by you. Always. I'll fight for you, with you, even when the world makes it hard. I'll try to be the man you deserve, even on the days when I'm not sure I know how. I'll love you in all the ways I can—loud, messy, fierce—because that's all I've got. You're it for me. Always have been, always will be."

His words, unpolished as they were, held a rawness that struck me deeply. It was not the poetry of old, of Philetos, but it was truth, and in truth, there was its own kind of beauty. My eyes stung with unshed tears, and as one escaped, trailing down my cheek, Silas reached up, brushing it away with the pad of his thumb, his touch as gentle as his words were rough.

"Silas," I began, my voice softer, quieter, but steady. "From the moment I met you, it was as though the world had shifted, realigned in ways I couldn't yet understand. You saw in me something I had long forgotten, a future I was not prepared for, a love I was unworthy of. Despite my mistakes, my walls I have built, you stayed. Steadfast and unwavering, and in doing so, you taught me that perhaps, in some way, I was meant for this—for us."

I could see the emotion flicker in his eyes, the vulnerability he so rarely let show, and it made me falter for just a moment. But I continued, my words slower, deliberate.

"Your love has been a storm, relentless and powerful, reshaping everything it touches. It broke through the walls I had built, and I found myself standing exposed, vulnerable, but never afraid. Not with you. In your arms, I have known peace, something I thought was lost to me. I promise to be the calm to your storm, the anchor when the tides rise too high. I promise to love you with quiet devotion, with patience, with reverence. I will cherish the fire in you. And I will love you endlessly through every joy and every hardship. You are my heart, my light, my home. And I am yours, for as long as we have."

His eyes, now glistening with unshed tears of his own, mirrored the depth of emotion in my chest. It made me want to reach out, to hold him close, to reassure him, though I knew his tears were not of sorrow but of love, of relief that this moment had finally come.

The priestess stepped forward, offering us the rings, simple golden bands, but heavy with the weight of what they signified. One by one, we placed them on each other's fingers, the cool metal a promise in itself.

"By the Gods' blessing, seal your vows with a kiss," the priestess intoned softly.

Without hesitation, Silas cupped my face in his hands, and I mirrored the gesture, our lips meeting in a kiss that was not merely a formality but a declaration—a promise.

This was it, the culmination of lifetimes, the binding of souls that had been waiting for this moment through endless cycles of loss and reunion. There's a quiet, unspoken beauty in growing old with the one you love—a beauty I never imagined I would be granted. If I'm honest, the thought had never even crossed my mind. Immortality doesn't lend itself to such considerations; you don't think of the end when you believe there isn't one. But now, standing on the edge of something finite, I find there is a kind of peace in it, a tenderness that comes with knowing our time is shared.

And in that, I am fortunate in a way even most mortals will never know.

NOTE FROM THE AUTHOR

I've always been captivated by the tragic tale of Orpheus and Eurydice, and it inspired me to write something that echoes its themes. Zayd was Philetos' muse, and then Silas'. If only Zayd hadn't looked back to his old love, if only he'd chosen to move forward. Their story might not have been in a cycle of tragedy. But love, entwined with obsession, often walks hand in hand with destruction.

This story also drew inspiration from a song I couldn't stop listening to for the longest time. I wanted to create a story that evoked the same emotions that song stirred in me: a connection that is both your greatest solace and your inevitable undoing. The line "Like a moth to a flame, I had been drawn to him, knowing that I was destined to burn" from BotF was deeply influenced by its lyrics.

Zayd and Philetos' story lived in my mind for a long time, and I truly hope you enjoyed reading it as much as I enjoyed bringing it to paper.

Thank you so much for reading my story! I'd be truly grateful if you could take a moment to leave an honest review and rating on Goodreads, Amazon, or any other platform you prefer. Your feedback makes a world of difference for small authors like me. If you'd like to learn more about me, explore my other works, or check out upcoming projects, please visit https://elijahher.com.

Thank you again for your support!

OTHER WORKS BY ELIJAH HER

"Ascendance of the Forgotten Prince"

An achillean novel about survival and reclamation as a magically-forgotten prince endures enslavement, political intrigue, and forbidden passion to reclaim his birthright.

"Her Majesty's Captain"

A sapphic novella about forging your own path, that is inspired by *The Princess Bride*. The story follows a princess and her presumably dead childhood best friend, who isn't actually dead and is now a pirate captain.

"Where the Tides Meet"

An achillean novel that is inspired by *The Little Mermaid*. The story follows a merfolk prince that dares to step onto land in search of vengeance. Yet what he finds is not the cruelty he was taught to hate, but a human who awakens in him a tenderness he never thought possible.

and a few web-novels that are only available on Tapas.

CHARACTERS OF BotF

Zayd (He/Him)

Age: Looks Late-20s

Sexual Orientation: Omnisexual

Species: Eudaimon

Personality Type & Sign: ISTJ, Capricorn

Physical Descriptions: Dark Blue Eyes, Raven Black Hair, 5'11" Athletic Build

Favorites: History, Art, Melomakarona, Vinsanto

Silas Vassallo (He/Him)

Age: 30

Sexual Orientation: Gay

Species: Human

Personality Type & Sign: ENTJ, Scorpio

Physical Descriptions: Brown Eyes, Sandy Blond Hair, Hand & Arm & Back Tattoo, 6'1" Athletic Build

Favorites: Whiskey, Chiffon Cake, Music, Romcoms

THE DAIMON WORLD OF BotF

The world of *Binds of the Forsaken* was inspired by Hellenic mythos surrounding Daemons and the multifaceted aspects of the Theoi, the gods.

In BotF, the Theion are the divine beings of creation, the gods. They are multifaceted, multi-gendered, and encompass all aspects of the universe and existence itself. Daimons are divine beings that influence mortals under the orders of the Theion. Their job is to maintain balance, chaos, and order. Eudaimons are meant to inspire, while Kakodaimons are meant to tempt. Neither is strictly good or bad, despite their own personal beliefs.

The divine realm is divided into three planes of mists. Aither is the realm of the Eudaimons and the Theion. Erebos is the realm of the Kakodaimons and the deceased. Khaos is the in-between; the dead pass through to get to Erebos, and the Daimons linger to watch over the mortal realm. In Khaos, the mists swirl through the land of the living unseen, unheard, undetected.

Mortal souls follow a cycle of rebirth, living new lives after death. The number of renewals is determined by the Theion, but all souls are finite. When their cycle ends, they are drawn to Erebos, where they rest in eternal limbo, endlessly reliving either their most cherished or most regretted moments.

Want more of the daimon universe? *Renascence of the Forsaken*, is a novella following the first reincarnation of Eryx of BotF as he navigates mortality and love. Coming early 2026.

A Daimon Short-Story

BINDS OF DESIRE

ELIJAH HER

NOTE FROM THE AUTHOR

Binds of Desire includes explicit sexual content and absolutely no plot.

Just a spicy short-story displaying an author's self indulgent "why choose" AU of their own work. Don't mind me. This is an alternative universe where a certain daimon didn't sacrifice himself, and a certain human isn't destined to die every time he meets his soulmate.

SILAS

The air was thick with its usual layers: the clinking of glass, the rise and fall of voices that veered from laughter to muttered complaints, the scent of liquor mingling with the kind of longing people bring to a place like this—a longing for relief, distraction, or something they couldn't name. I longed for a place such as this too, which was why I carved it out to be my sanctuary. My retreat. *Tregua nascosta.*

The door cracked open with a whisper of the night air, the chill cutting through the heat of bodies and beer, and there he was again. Like clockwork. Always. The man with raven-dark hair, black as a starless sky, and eyes that unsettled something in me every time. *Mar d'inverno*, I thought. The winter sea. Not just blue, but deep, fathomless, the kind of blue that would pull you under before you realized you'd stopped breathing. I had seen countless men and women come through these doors, their beauty gilded by dim lights and tequila shots, and none of them had ever hit me the way he did. A punch to the gut I didn't see coming.

His face carried such a haunting melancholy, as if he had been bearing the weight of a thousand unsaid things. It stirred something primal in me—an overwhelming urge to pin him down, to steal him from his torment, to shatter that endless storm of thoughts. I wanted to unravel him, piece by piece, until every shred of frustration was replaced by me. Until his mind broke and I was all that was left—his anchor, his chaos, his sanctuary.

The thought burned low in my chest, scalding me. I hated it as much as I needed it.

"Instead of staring at him all the time, why don't you just go talk to him?" Ivy's voice broke through my thoughts like a rock through glass. She bumped her hip into mine with that smug little grin, and beer sloshed over the lip of the glass onto my hand before I caught it.

"Pretty sure he has a boyfriend," I muttered, voice clipped as I wiped my damp fingers on a rag and turned toward the bar. I pulled a smile from where I kept the customer service ones, all teeth and cheer. "Here you go. Enjoy."

Ivy, of course, was relentless. "You *think* he has a boyfriend," she mused later, as the music throbbed low enough to cover our voices. She perched herself on a stool, feet dangling like a kid's. "But do you *know* for sure? It's not like they're making out in front of you."

I didn't answer, not at first. My eyes had already drifted back, as if compelled, to the far corner where he always sat. A sanctuary within my sanctuary. And like some cursed kind of clockwork, the other man appeared beside him, the one who never failed to send a tight coil of tension through my gut. He reminded me too much of where I came from, of the cold pressure of a knife in a darkened alley or the weight of a name that didn't belong to me anymore. Legare.

"See?" I said finally, jaw set as I nodded toward the pair.

Ivy waved off my words with a flick of her hand. "So? Could be a fling. Friends with benefits. Just friends. Just benefits." Her tone turned teasing as she tilted her head to grin at me. "You need one of those. When was the last time you had any fun? Oh, look!"

I turned my head just in time to see a drunk patron stumble, colliding into him. A drink splattered across his shoulder, dark against darker fabric. He rose from his seat, that melancholy face slipping into a practiced smile. Reassuring. Unbothered.

"Go save him," Ivy said, her voice suddenly sharper with excitement. "Charm him. You're good at that."

I turned back to her with a look that might have been a glare if I weren't so tired.

"Silas," she said, drawing out my name like she was mocking me, like she saw straight through to the part of me that wanted it—that wanted *him*.

I looked back.

He was still there, shaking his head slightly as if trying to laugh it off. His companion leaned closer to murmur something low in his ear, and I didn't know why but I wanted to know what was said to elicit that defiant yet playful roll of his eyes. Another part of me also wanted to watch his eyes roll back in other ways.

My fingers flexed against the bar top. I felt myself pulled, the need thrumming in my chest like some goddamn war drum. *"Fuck it,"* I sighed internally. She was right. This was the perfect moment, and I seized it, even though my stomach twisted at the thought of making a fool of myself. My fingers closed around a clean hand towel, the soft cotton rough against the calluses of my palms, and before I could think twice, I stepped out from behind the bar. My pace was quick, maybe too quick, but I needed to act before the moment slipped through my fingers.

"Hey, I'm sorry about that." The words came out in a rush as I stopped in front of him, extending the towel toward him like it was some kind of olive branch. He turned to look at me, slow and deliberate, his dark lashes casting shadows over the curve of his cheek. His expression was calm, a faint smile tugging at his lips, though it didn't quite reach his eyes.

"It's no problem," he said, his voice smooth, low, and measured. "It's a bar. Can't expect everyone to handle their liquor."

"Yeah, but I'm the bartender," I said, chuckling softly, though the sound felt hollow to my own ears. "It's my job to cut them off and avoid these kinds of messes."

He took the towel, his movements precise, careful as he dabbed at the fabric of his button-up. The dark stain of the spilled drink clung to him like some kind of bruise, a mark that didn't belong. His gaze flicked downward, following the motion of his hands, and silence settled between us.

I should've left. I knew it, and so did he. This was the point where the interaction was supposed to end—a polite exchange, a shared laugh, and then I'd walk away, back to the safety of the bar and the steady rhythm of my usual routine. But

I could feel Ivy's eyes on me from across the room, sharp and encouraging, her unspoken dare hanging heavy in the air.

"I'm also the owner," I said, my voice steadier than I expected, though the words felt clumsy, like they didn't quite belong in my mouth. "So it's my job to make it up to a patron when they have a less-than-savory encounter. Let me get you a drink. On the house."

His gaze lifted then, meeting mine, and for a moment, the world seemed to hold its breath. There was something unreadable in those eyes, something soft and yet felt like a weight pressed against my ribs, heavy and impossible to name.

My attention flickered to his companion, seated across from him in the booth. The man was a stark contrast to the quiet melancholy of the one in front of me—relaxed, self-assured, his arms stretched across the back of the booth like he owned the place. His dark gray eyes caught the low light, sharp and amused, as if he could see right through me, stripping me down to something raw and vulnerable. There was something predatory in his gaze, not unkind but knowing, like he was already a step ahead of me, watching to see what I'd do next.

"Come up to the bar," I said, forcing my gaze back to the man in front of me, though I could still feel the other's presence like a shadow. "Both of you. I'll give you a round."

ERYX

"He likes you," I said, a grin curling at the edges of my mouth, the leather seat beneath me groaning in protest as I rose. I stretched lazily, enjoying the slight tension in my limbs as I watched Zayd methodically blot the beer from his shirt.

"Of course he does," he replied, his tone even, almost dismissive, as though he were stating a fact as simple as the sky being blue. He didn't look at me, his focus fixed on the damp fabric beneath his fingers. "He's supposed to."

I tilted my head, studying him with a bemused expression. "I think it's more than that," I said lightly, though there was weight behind my words, a gentle but persistent nudge.

After everything—after the first reincarnation, the second, and all the ones that followed—he still clung to this stubborn denial. As if the raw, genuine feelings Philetos wore so plainly were nothing more than echoes of obligation by the divine. He'd never admit it but I knew it for what it was. A defense mechanism, sharp-edged and deliberate, meant to keep the cracks from showing. A fear, deep-seated and stubborn, that all this pain and sorrow, this endless, merciless cycle between them, was one-sided. That it was only him, always him, who truly felt the weight of those feelings. It would make it easier for him—hurt less—if he ever discovered that notion to be true. Convincing himself of it now, before the truth had the chance to wound him.

"Yeah," he said, his bluntness cutting clean through the air, "he's probably just horny."

I laughed, a soft chuckle that rolled out of me before I could stop it. We began to make our way toward the bar, the hum of the room around us growing louder with each step. My fingers found their way to the back of his hair, teasing gently at the strands. "Is there a problem with that?" I asked, my tone playful, though the question carried a thread of seriousness beneath it. "You know that not everything has to be romantic."

I watched him out of the corner of my eye, his profile as steady and composed as it always was. But as we neared the counter, there it was again—that flicker, the faint but unmistakable glimmer of something softer lighting up his face. It happened only in moments like this, when he allowed himself to step closer to his human. It was beautiful in a way that felt almost painful to watch, like sunlight breaking through the cracks of a storm-ravaged sky. If I had my way, I'd lock them in a room together and keep them there, free from interference. I'd drag the whole world away from their door and let him have what he was too stubborn to take.

But Zayd would kill me if I did, and Silas probably wouldn't appreciate captivity either. I'd been told, after all, that confinement doesn't sit well with humans.

Zayd leaned his forearms against the dark, weathered wood of the bar, and Silas stepped forward to greet him, his smile just crooked enough to be infuriatingly charming. There was something begrudging in the way he carried it, like he was well aware of the effect it had on people and resigned to it.

"What'll it be?" Silas asked, his voice smooth, a low murmur that felt like an invitation even when he didn't mean it to. His gaze shifted briefly to me, and I caught the faintest flicker of assessment in his dark brown eyes before they snapped back to Zayd. For a moment, silence stretched between them—loaded, sharp, as if the weight of something unspoken hung in the air between their glances.

I nearly rolled my eyes and resisted the urge to groan aloud. Sexual tension this thick could suffocate a man, and I wasn't the only one who noticed. The red-haired bartender behind Silas cast a knowing glance in their direction, her smile teasing as though she was about to say something but thought better of it.

I couldn't help myself. "He'll take a Brandy Alexander, and I'll have an Amaretto Sour," I said, cutting clean through the moment. Someone had to. And supposedly saying 'just go fuck already' isn't appropriate.

Silas arched a brow at Zayd, waiting for confirmation. Zayd gave a dignified nod. "On it," Silas said. He reached for the glasses with practiced ease, his movements fluid, deliberate. The bar's low lighting caught the amber glint of the brandy as he poured it, the curve of the glass catching shadows and light as he worked. Silas moved like someone who knew exactly what he was doing—not just with the drinks, but with the space he occupied, the way he filled it effortlessly. He crushed ice with the rhythm of someone who could do this blindfolded, his fingers deft as he poured, shook, and stirred. Silas was hot. Even I couldn't deny that.

Finally, he slid the drinks toward us with a flourish, a flicker of satisfaction on his face. "There you go," he said, his tone casual, but his eyes flicked to Zayd once more.

And Zayd, ever composed, ever maddeningly polite, lifted his glass with the faintest curve of his lips. "Thank you," he said calm and coolly.

"I've seen you and your boyfriend come in often," Silas said, his voice smooth. There was a deliberate pause, a window wide enough for Zayd to correct him, though of course, Zayd didn't. "But I don't think I've had the pleasure of serving either of you. Usually it was Ivy, right?" He nodded toward the red-haired bartender, her laugh cutting softly through the noise behind him as she spoke to a customer.

By the gods, did I have to do everything myself? I set my glass down, the faint tang of the Amaretto Sour lingering on my tongue, sweet and sharp. "Not boyfriends," I said finally, drawing the words out like an exhale, the impatience curling in my chest though I hid it under a smile. If I had to sit through this charade any longer, I'd drink the whole damn bar dry—and even then, there wouldn't be enough liquor in this place to get a Daimon drunk. This, right here, was why I didn't bother tagging along for these things. I wasn't built for wingman duty, despite the irony of my wings.

I leaned back, glancing at Zayd with a faint smirk as I added, "Though I'm sure he's looking for one." The words fell off my tongue like a challenge or invitation. I tipped my empty glass toward Silas and held up two fingers. "Two more, please."

Silas raised an eyebrow, the barest flicker of concern shadowing his expression, but Zayd stepped in with that calm, measured tone of his. "He can handle his liquor," Zayd said with a low chuckle, the sound soft and placating.

Silas lingered a moment longer, then took my glass and stepped away, leaving the air between us heavier than it had been.

"What are you doing?" Zayd asked, his voice hushed, his shoulder leaning into me as though the weight of his words demanded secrecy. His brows knitted together, his tone sharper, though still quiet enough that the music swallowed most of the bite.

I turned toward him, letting the faintest smirk curl my lips, leaning closer until my breath brushed the shell of his ear. "What am I doing? What are you doing?" My voice dropped low, teasing, because teasing was easier than scolding, easier than shaking him and telling him to get over himself. "Is this really how you flirt? You've had centuries, little Eudai. Centuries. You'd think you'd be better at this by now."

He tensed beside me, and for a second I thought I'd insulted him. But then he sighed, long and slow, and the tension bled from his shoulders. "It's not that simple," he murmured, his voice softer now. "He looks so much like him."

I tilted my head, studying him, the quiet sadness coiled behind his words. I didn't let it last long. "Eh," I said with a grin. "I think this version's hotter."

Zayd shot me a look but there was something softer beneath it—a flicker of exasperation laced with amusement. His lips quirked, almost imperceptibly, as if betraying the faintest ghost of a smile.

"So, you're looking for a boyfriend?" Silas set the glasses down, the mischief in his words belying the steady weight of his gaze.

Zayd shook his head lightly, the movement subtle, measured, as if even the gesture had to carry the grace of a man who was never rushed, never undone. A small smile tugged at the corners of his mouth as he lifted his glass, pausing just long enough to murmur, "I suppose I am, yes," before taking a slow sip.

Silas leaned forward, his elbows brushing the worn wood of the bar, his brown eyes holding steady on Zayd, their warmth darkened now by a flicker of something bolder. A look I knew all too well. "I could be your boyfriend," he said, the words falling from his lips. "Even if it's just for the night."

There was no hesitance in his tone, no coyness, only the kind of confidence that came from a man who didn't just know his power but wielded it like an art form. His smile deepened as he added, "My place isn't far. You can even bring your not-boyfriend," he said, his gaze flicking to me for the briefest moment, before returning to Zayd, steady and expectant. "I don't mind an audience."

I raised an eyebrow, biting back the laugh that threatened to escape. Wingman to voyeur. It wasn't what I had expected for the night, but then again, expectations had always been overrated.

"What'll it be, handsome?" Silas' voice dropped lower now, the smooth edge of it curling into something darker. He leaned further across the counter, his lids lowering, a glint of lust sharpening his gaze as he added, "Want a boyfriend or two for the night?"

ZAYD

To say it was awkward would be a simplification, though the word itself felt shallow against the storm of emotions that churned beneath the surface. In all our time together, in all the centuries and reincarnations, the thought of this moment had never occurred to me—not in the shape it had now taken. At first, there had been guilt, a sharp-edged thing, for seeking solace with Eryx in Philetos' absence, but that guilt had softened over time, dulled into an unspoken understanding between us. Eryx never asked for explanations or conditions, and I never offered them. What existed between us was unspoken, its edges worn smooth by years of quiet acceptance. But with Philetos—Silas—there had never been space to speak of such things, let alone to introduce them.

And yet, here we were.

Silas lifted me onto the wooden countertop. He stood between my legs, his body warm and steady, his hands threading through my hair as though he had every right to claim it, every right to hold me in place. He kissed with the urgency of someone who never feared rejection, the taste of whiskey and smoke lingering on his lips, earthy and dark. There was a roughness to his movements, a kind of unpolished hunger that made my pulse quicken despite myself. But even as his body pressed close to mine, I could not stop my gaze from drifting, slipping past him to where Eryx sat, a presence as undeniable as the air in the room.

Eryx lounged on the leather sofa in the corner of Silas' studio apartment, his body draped in that effortless way of his. The drink in his hand caught the faint, warm light from the single lamp, and he tilted the glass slightly, the liquid inside golden. His gaze never wavered, fixed on me with a calm, unwavering intensity. He didn't smile, not fully, but there was something in his eyes—amusement, perhaps, or curiosity. Maybe even something deeper, though Eryx rarely gave away enough to be certain.

The space itself was far too modest for privacy. A single room, save for the bathroom, its furniture sparse and practical. The kitchen bled into the living area, and the bed was pressed against a wall as though trying to make itself small. It was far removed from the opulence Silas could command if he chose to. A mafia prince, and this was where he lived—above a bar, tucked into anonymity.

I felt Silas pause, his lips hovering just above mine, the weight of my distraction not lost on him. He tilted his head slightly, catching the direction of my gaze before his own flickered to Eryx. His expression shifted, a subtle smirk pulling at the corner of his mouth as he looked back at me. His approval was unspoken but clear, a flicker of heat in his eyes that said he understood what I desired.

"Eryx," I said at last, the name slipping from my lips steady and measured, betraying none of the turmoil that stirred beneath. My voice was calm, too calm for the wild thrum of my heartbeat. I had no need to say more. Eryx understood me better than most, and he had long ago learned to read what was not said.

He set his drink down with a quiet finality, the glass meeting the coffee table with a soft clink. Rising from the sofa, he moved with that familiar, deliberate grace, his steps slow but purposeful. The leather creaked faintly as he left it behind, the sound lost beneath the weight of his presence as he crossed the floor toward us.

Silas shifted, stepping back just enough to make room, his gaze flickering between us as though anticipating the next moment with something close to delight. My fingers lingered on the fabric of his shirt, preventing him from going far, even as my focus shifted partially to Eryx.

My other hand found its way to the back of Eryx's hair, fingers tangling in the soft strands as I drew him closer. Our lips met in a collision of heat and urgency, his kiss bold and unyielding. His hand pressed against the countertop for balance as he leaned into me, his body answering mine with instinctive fervor. A shiver traced down my spine as I felt the faint, deliberate graze of Silas' lips against my neck, his breath warm and teasing, his hand trailing upward along my thigh with maddening slowness. The growing ache beneath my clothes was undeniable, my arousal straining against the confines of fabric, demanding release.

Then came the sudden chill of the air against my skin as Silas freed me, his hand curling around my cock with a deliberate slowness that was equal parts torment and pleasure. My breath hitched as he stroked me, each motion precise, his touch as confident as the rest of him. And then, the warmth of his mouth, hot and wet as it slid over me, sent a jolt of sensation that left me gripping the countertop for stability.

Eryx broke the kiss, his gaze flickering downward as though drawn by an invisible tether to the sight of Silas, lips stretched around my girth, moving with a rhythm that was both maddening and exquisite. I saw the shift in Eryx's expression as it changed into something more primal, more intent. His hand moved to Silas' hair, guiding him in a way that spoke of long-forged familiarity, knowing precisely what I liked without words. Gently guiding him faster, deeper, along my cock.

My hands braced against the countertop as I leaned back, surrendering to the cascade of pleasure, my lips parting as soft, guttural sounds escaped me. Silas' gaze lifted, his eyes locking with mine, a silent assertion of control that sent another wave of heat coursing through me. He was magnetic, irresistible, and he knew it, every movement of his tongue deliberate, calculated to draw out my undoing.

Then his attention shifted, sliding to Eryx with a look that could have melted iron. He reached up, his fingers curling in the fabric of Eryx's shirt, pulling him down with a force that left no room for misinterpretation. And Eryx closed the distance without hesitation.

My pulse quickened as I watched them, their shared focus creating an intimacy that was almost sacred. They moved together with a synchronicity that spoke of unspoken understanding, their lips slick with spit and lust as they took turns on me, their mouths working in harmony that bordered on reverence. It felt excessive, indulgent in a way that should have felt sinful but instead left me drunk on the attention, their touch and taste igniting a fire that burned through every inch of me. But it wasn't enough—I wanted more. I shifted, my hands moving to rest on each of their faces, the warmth of their skin grounding me even as the desire between us threatened to unmoor me entirely.

Gently, I guided their faces toward each other, the motion slow and deliberate, a quiet command that required no words. Their lips met without hesitation, the kiss fevered and unrelenting, and I couldn't help but marvel at the sight of them losing themselves in each other. It was beautiful in its rawness, a moment that felt both eternal and fleeting, a collision of passion and need that left me breathless.

My hand drifted downward, wrapping around myself as I began to stroke, the slickness of their combined spit adding a tantalizing edge to every movement. I watched them, utterly captivated by the way they moved together, their shared desire spilling over and wrapping around me like a living thing. This was indulgence, yes—overindulgence, perhaps—but in that moment, it felt like the only thing that mattered, a communion of touch and want that left no room for doubt or regret.

"You're enjoying this too much. Who knew you could be such a pervert?" Eryx's voice carried that teasing lilt. A crooked smile tugged at his lips, yet there was something more in his tone—playfulness edged with heat. He pulled away from Silas with a swift motion, his movements smooth as water, and before I could fully process it, I was lifted and dropped onto Silas' bed. The mattress gave a soft creak beneath me.

Silas leaned over me, the corner of his mouth quirking upward as he began tugging his shirt over his head. "It's hot, sure, watching us go at it. But I think it'd be even hotter if we both had you between us, Zay." His words came rough, low, as if scraped from the back of his throat, and I could feel the weight of his gaze as it roamed over me, dark and expectant.

Eryx began undoing the buttons of his shirt, his fingers unhurried but sure, deft in their purpose. One by one, the small fastenings gave way until the fabric slid from his shoulders, pooling at his feet like discarded silk. The dim light caught on the sharp planes of his chest, the curve of muscle, the tattoos that adorned his skin. He stood at the edge of the bed, his hand moving slowly over himself, the motion languid and deliberate as though every stroke was meant to be watched, savored.

Silas kneeled next to me, his hands quick but not careless as he helped me out of my clothes, each tug and pull a wordless declaration of urgency, as if waiting another moment might undo him entirely. The air brushed cool against my skin as more of me was revealed, but it wasn't long before the heat of him replaced it.

I was pliant beneath him, moved without resistance, as though I were no more than a vessel for his desires, caught in the tide of his touch. Silas tugged at my calves, spreading me open with an unceremonious ease, and the shift sent my back sinking deeper into the mattress. My body, already taut with anticipation, trembled as he leaned down, the heat of his breath brushing against my skin, my cock twitching, eager, only to be startled by the unexpected. A warm wetness, intimate and unrelenting, traced the sensitive edges of my hole.

The shock of it made me look down, my gaze traveling over the length of my body, only to find Silas knelt between my legs, his head bowed as though in reverence, his brown eyes looking up too me through dark lashes. His tongue worked against me, slow and insistent, each flick igniting a spark that burned away the last traces of shame. Heat bloomed across my face, a flush that threatened to drown me in its intensity, but there was no refuge, no retreat. Not when the embarrassment gave way to the sharp edge of pleasure as his tongue retreated, replaced by the deliberate push of his finger.

I moaned, my head tilting instinctively as my fingers dug into the sheets to anchor myself. Eryx's hand, gentle but firm cupped my jaw, guiding me to look up to meet his gaze, to surrender to him. His thumb brushed my cheek, slow and affectionate, a contrast to the boldness of his next move. The head of his cock, thick and flushed, pressed against my lips, leaving a bead of wetness behind. "Open up, my little Eudai," he murmured, his voice a low sultry purr.

Silas' fingers moved with a maddening precision, their rhythm a silent challenge, a teasing demand that matched the pace of my lips as I took Eryx deeper. It was a game, unspoken, an intricate balance of give and take. If I wanted to feel more, to drown in their attention, I had to offer it in kind. My mouth worked over Eryx's cock, the heat and weight of him filling me, my tongue tracing every ridge, every vein as though committing it to memory. He let out a low, unguarded sigh, his fingers threading through my hair, his touch light yet insistent as he grasped the nape of my neck.

The heaviness in my balls became a persistent ache, building deep and low until it pressed against the edges of my restraint. My toes curled as Silas' fingers slid deeper inside me, stretching, coaxing, the friction pulling a shudder from my body. His tongue darted over the sensitive underside of my shaft, a fleeting touch that ignited a fire I could no longer contain. The tension in my thighs coiled and snapped, and I moaned, guttural and raw, the sound muffled against the thick heat of Eryx's cock.

Cum spilled from me, wave after wave, thick and hot. Silas' fingers pushed faster against my sensitive walls, refusing to let me come down. He chased every last pulse of my release, drawing it out with a determination that bordered on cruelty, each sensation sharpened by his refusal to relent. My body trembled beneath his touch, my breath ragged, the remnants of my orgasm still echoing through me like the aftershocks of a storm. Eryx's hand tightened briefly in my hair, grounding me, his steady presence a contrast to Silas' unyielding intensity. Together, they unraveled me completely.

ERYX

Theions... He was so hot. For all his haughtiness and those bouts of tightly wound propriety, there was no denying the way he unraveled when he gave in to pleasure, no mistaking the sweet vulnerability that slipped past his usual reserve. My fingers grazed the sharp line of his cheekbone, tracing down to the edge of his jaw as he licked a slow, deliberate line along the side of my cock. It was maddening, the teasing motion, the way his tongue lingered just enough to send a shiver down my spine but refused me the release I so desperately needed. I'd almost came three times already, and he knew it... *brat.* My head fell back against the mattress, a sharp exhale leaving me as my cock twitched under his attention. *The shit I do for you,* I thought, my lips curved into a grin I couldn't quite suppress, *and this is how you repay me.*

Zayd knelt between my legs, braced on all fours, his forearms resting against my legs. Behind him, Silas knelt with a bottle of lube in one hand, his cock in the other, an easy smirk tugging at the corners of his mouth.

Finally, Zayd took me back into the wet heat of his mouth, and my body tensed in anticipation. His lips stretched around me, his tongue tracing along the sensitive underside as he worked me deeper. My fingers found their way to his dark hair, sliding through the strands before tightening with a low moan.

I could tell when Silas entered him—Zayd froze, his lips parting against me, a soft, involuntary gasp escaping as his body adjusted to the intrusion. His fingers gripped my thighs harder, the edges of his nails biting into my skin, a fleeting contrast of pleasure and pain. He paused, still as a statue, caught between sensation and silence, leaving me stranded on the cusp of my own release.

"Uh-uh," I murmured, my voice rough, a half-teasing, half-commanding whisper. My grip in his hair tightened, and with a single, deliberate motion, I pushed his head back down onto my cock.

"Fuck, your body takes to me so easily," Silas murmured, his voice thick with desire, his gaze dark and heavy-lidded as his hands gripped Zayd's hips, keeping him pinned firmly in place.

I leaned back, the corners of my mouth curling into a lazy, almost feral smile, watching the way Zayd's flushed skin glistened with exertion, the way the tremor in his limbs betrayed the strain of being pulled apart and claimed by both of us. "You were right," I said, my voice holding a teasing edge. "He does look good between us."

Zayd's lips were swollen, slick with spit, his chin wet where it had dripped down in glistening rivulets. His body strained as he moved between us, caught in the rhythm of Silas thrusting into him and me filling his mouth. A bloom of crimson spread across his chest and neck.

Silas slowed his movements, his hips rocking gently as he glanced up to meet my eyes over Zayd's trembling frame.

"Eryx." My name was a breath, cool and weighted, even through the haze of his arousal. His lips parted as if to say more, but instead, he moved, leaning forward and reaching out. His fingers brushed against mine, removing my grip in Zayd's hair to replace it with his own. Silas gripped his hair and tugged him upright with an easy dominance.

Zayd didn't resist. He moved forward without complaint, his hands bracing against my chest as Silas pulled out and made him move to straddle me. His eyes were half-lidded, hazy with lust, but there was something unshakable in his gaze, something that always made my breath catch when he looked at me like that. Slowly, Zayd reached behind himself, guiding me into him, his brows drawing together in a fleeting moment of resistance before his body gave way.

My hands found his hips as he sank down fully, sheathing me within him. His breath hitched, his shoulders trembling, but he held my gaze, unwavering. *Do you know what you do to me?* Fuck, how easily he unravels me. Oh how I would have given anything just to keep him looking at me like that. His palm cupped my face, and his lips brushed against mine, soft at first, then deepening, hungry and urgent. Heat coiled low in my testicles, aching and insistent, but I tightened my grip on his backside, holding him still, forcing him to slow.

"You feel so fucking good," I whispered against his lips, my voice rough and unguarded.

Then I felt it—another set of hands, firm and deliberate, sliding up my thighs. Silas. "I think Zayd can take more," he said, his voice a low, velvety murmur. His eyes flicked to Zayd, watching him with a sharp, almost predatory focus. "What do you think, Zayd? Do you think you can handle both of us?"

Zayd's answer came without hesitation, a breathless, broken "yes" against my lips, and that was all the invitation Silas needed.

I felt the press of Silas' cock alongside mine, the stretch of Zayd's body as he took us both. His muscles clenched around us, tight and overwhelming, a perfect pressure that made my head fall back with a groan. The sensation was maddening, exhilarating, our cocks pressed flush against each other, moving in sync inside of Zayd.

"Your body was made to take us," I murmured, the words slipping out in a low purr. My hands slid up his sweat-slicked back, holding him closer. There was something holy in the way he looked, undone and radiant. If the Theions and Daimons could see him now, they would call it blasphemy. But to me, he had never looked more divine.

Zayd's body trembled one last time, a shuddering gasp escaping him as his cum spilled over my stomach. His muscles clenched around both Silas and me. The pressure, the heat, was almost too much to bear; it felt like my dick was going to snap off. My orgasm followed fast on the heels of his, tearing through me like a tide that had been held back too long. I could feel the thrum of Silas' climax against mine, the rhythm of it merging with my own.

And then it was over. Zayd collapsed onto me, his body spent and pliant, his breath uneven as it ghosted over my skin.

Silas moved to lie beside us, and Zayd shifted instinctively, draping his arm over Silas' chest, drawing him nearer. The room was silent except for the sound of our breathing, ragged at first, then slowing into something soft and steady. The air was thick with the scent of us.

It was Silas who broke the silence, his voice low but edged with humor. "Boyfriend for just the night, right?"

I laughed softly, my chest vibrating beneath Zayd's weight. "I think we all know this is more than just one night." I murmured, reaching out to brush aside the blond hair that clung to his forehead.

Silas chuckled, the sound rich and warm, and Zayd stirred between us, lifting a hand to gently cup the side of Silas' face. His thumb moved in slow, deliberate strokes over Silas' cheek.

In that moment, there was no need for words. There was something satisfying in the way our pleasures had intertwined, in the way we had all played a part for one another, filling spaces we hadn't even realized were empty. Alone, any one of us might have been enough, but together we were something fuller. This wasn't just one night. Not when we fit together like this.

www.ingramcontent.com/pod-product-compliance
Lightning Source LLC
Chambersburg PA
CBHW020416110726
47899CB00006B/2011